ORPHAN AHWAK

Raquel Rivera

ORCA BOOK PUBLISHERS

Library and Archives Canada Cataloguing in Publication

Rivera, Raquel, 1966-
Orphan Ahwak / written by Raquel Rivera.

ISBN 978-1-55143-653-1

I. Title.

PS8635.I9435O76 2007   jC813'.6   C2007-902769-5

First published in the United States, 2007

Library of Congress Control Number: 2007927582

Summary: Orphan Ahwak is determined to become a hunter and to find a place
in an often hostile and terrifying world.

Orca Book Publishers gratefully acknowledges the support for its publishing programs
provided by the following agencies: the Government of Canada through the Book
Publishing Industry Development Program and the Canada Council for the Arts,
and the Province of British Columbia through the BC Arts Council
and the Book Publishing Tax Credit.

Cover and text design by Teresa Bubela
Cover artwork by Germaine Arnaktauyok
Author photo by Kim Chua

ORCA BOOK PUBLISHERS
PO Box 5626, STN. B
VICTORIA, BC CANADA
V8R 6S4

ORCA BOOK PUBLISHERS
PO Box 468
CUSTER, WA USA
98240-0468

www.orcabook.com
Printed and bound in Canada.
Printed on 100% PCW paper.
10 09 08 07 • 4 3 2 1

For Nemo and Beru

Contents

Dead

FLOATING. BOBBING.

The water fit around her body. It held her up. She'd never been so comfortable in all her life. The sun warmed her face. She could see its orange glow, even though her eyes were shut. The glow pushed away the black.

The black? Oh no, the black!

Aneze splashed and gasped. She choked on water. She started to sink. She hit the rocky bottom of the creek. The creek! They must have thrown her into the creek.

She opened her eyes and turned her head—carefully now, it hurt. She could see Itiwan, her brother's best friend. He floated facedown. The back of his head was all pulpy. They'd smashed it with a war club. It all came rushing back to Aneze now.

War cries. Screaming. Her whole family tumbling out from under the sleeping furs. It was not yet dawn.

They hadn't even got their clothes on yet. But the enemy was upon them. Outside the tent, Aneze saw her friend, Tsedi, running away. They grabbed Tsedi by the hair. Tsedi's father was on the ground, twisting and thrashing. He didn't make a sound because of the arrow in his throat.

Aneze groaned with remembering. Her head felt as if it was going to drop off. Pain lashed down her neck and along her back. Oh, she remembered now. It was because of him, the warrior with the black-painted cheek. He must have smacked her head and knocked her out.

When he had first grabbed her, Aneze had screamed and cursed him. He just laughed. But he didn't see her knife. She swung out and caught him across the face—right through his paint, right through his eye, she hoped. He stopped laughing then. He twisted her hand until she felt a *snap*. Her knife fell to the ground. She tried to spit in his face, right into the wound, just to show him how despicable he was.

That's when he had cursed her, grabbed her up by the ankles and swung her like a toy doll.

Gently, Aneze lifted her hand up. It looked bad. It had swollen in the water. She moved her legs among the stones. They trembled, but they were still good. She started to sit up. Ohhh—that hurt! Maybe better to just lie here in the creek for a while. She turned her head—slowly. She took a drink. Then the pictures started coming. She didn't like it, but they came anyway, those pictures in her mind.

Brother's face, looking surprised, even after the war ax took off his head. Blood splattering across the family tent. Her father screaming with rage. The bad magic in the enemies' arrows froze his arms and legs first, then his throat, then his heart. Did Father see that they had got Mother too? Did he see her tied by the arms and neck? Was she being taken to be a wife for one of the enemies? Or would they kill her, just for fun, later on?

Aneze wished the pictures would go away. Maybe the black would come back. It hurt too much to be with the sun. Water sprang from her eyes. She looked over at Itiwan.

"I'm not crying," she told his poor battered head. "I'm just resting while I recover from my wounds."

Alive

THE COALS were still warm by the cooking pots.

It was near dark when Aneze dragged herself back to camp. She didn't want to come here. She didn't want to see her family, her friends—not like that. But she needed the food. And she needed the fire. Soon the animals would be drawn by the death-smell.

Aneze held her bad hand up to bring the swelling down. With her other hand she took a stick and poked the fire. She brought the sparks back to life. She fed the fire dry twigs and leaves. There was soup left in an over-turned pot. She checked through the camp. Maybe someone was left. Maybe someone else was alive.

Kegui's baby had been thrown against a rock. They must have taken Kegui, the way they took Mother. Brother and Father were still lying there, just the way Aneze remembered. *Look away, look away.*

But that didn't help. She saw them in her head. Father and Brother—they'd been so good, so strong! Her legs shook beneath her. Her heart thumped in her ears. Black was closing in. Aneze sat down, hard.

Slowly the black pushed back to the edges. She could see again. There was Tsedi. So they had killed her, in the end. The others were here too. The elders, the hunters, the children and the babies—all were dead. The women were gone. Maybe the enemies had come to get more wives for themselves.

Aneze was the only one left. If only she hadn't tried to spit in that enemy's face, she might have been taken as well. She might be with her mother and the other women now.

Aneze wasn't hungry, but she quickly drank the soup, all of it. For a moment she thought that her stomach would vomit it back out. But she hung on to it. She needed her strength back. She needed to think.

First of all, she had to leave this place quickly. It was full of angry spirits now. It was not a good place. Also, the bodies would draw Wolverine. She needed to go some-place safer…but where? The fire was here in camp.

The tree. It would have to be the tree for tonight. Aneze went into her family's tent and gathered up all the sinew ropes she could find. She needed the strong ones that Mother used to tie bundles to her back.

These would hold her. She tied them together to make one long rope. She also took her caribou blanket, rolled it up and tied it to her waist. She took one last look around. Anything else? Oh yes. She eased the hunting knife out of her brother's cold hand. Just in case. Then she held on to the hand. It was part of Brother, and she tried to honor it.

Last night, before falling asleep, Brother had promised to take her to a secret waterfall. He said it fell like a ray of sunlight. He said that Fish leaped out of the shining fall and dove into the green pool below.

"But don't tell," he warned her. "Itiwan doesn't want us to show it to anyone, especially not girls."

Aneze wouldn't have told, not ever.

But she must try to stop moaning now—what a crybaby she was. That's what Brother called her sometimes, and he was right. Get up. Hurry now, the light was gone. Get into the tree—quickly.

Aneze threw the long sinew rope up over the lowest branch of the great spruce tree. In other times this would have been perfect for a rope swing. Now she tied the two ends. Climbing would be hard with only one good hand. She tested her knot. It should hold. She grabbed both traces with her good hand and put her foot on the knot at the bottom. She hoisted herself up. The loop twisted and turned, but she hung on. There.

Now she was off the ground. The loop brought her close enough to the lowest branch. She could grab it and walk up the trunk with her feet. The only problem was that she needed both hands to do this. It couldn't be helped.

Aneze took a deep breath for courage and grabbed the branch with both hands. Lightning bolts of pain shot down her arm to her elbow. But the hand held firm. This was good news. She waited a moment to get used to the pain. Then she swung out one foot, then the other, as high as she could. One step up the trunk and her feet were gripping the branch. Pulling herself up with her good side, she twisted herself up. She was sitting on the branch.

"Ow! Ow! Ow! *OWWW*!" She checked her hand. If anything, it seemed a little better for the exercise. Could it be that it wasn't broken? What a stroke of luck that would be. She flexed it. She touched the red angry swelling. Tomorrow she would find Mother's medicine bag and wrap the hand.

Mother. Where was Mother now? Did she miss her girl-child? Aneze blinked. She felt her eyes sting; her throat swelled. She pulled up the rope and tied herself to the tree for the night.

AT FIRST LIGHT, Aneze untied herself from the tree and hang-dropped to the ground. She hadn't slept much. "Rest is almost as good as sleep," she told herself. She had heard Wolverine in the night, feasting on the bodies. She made sure not to look at them this morning. She needed to gather a bundle and leave this place. She should have left yesterday.

She found dried caribou meat in Tsedi's tent. She found her mother's medicine bag, its contents strewn under the tumbled sleeping furs in her own family's tent. Her hand was a little better. Was it root she needed or leaves? Use both, she decided. After some mashing and crushing, Aneze covered her hand with the pulp. She found a rag to tie over it and keep it in place. That ought to do it.

Now she needed to find a flint stone. "A flint stone is a woman's most important possession," Mother had told her once. Aneze knew her mother's flint stone would not be in the tent. Mother always kept it close, tied somewhere on her body, wherever she was. Women wore them even to sleep. They hid them from Wolverine, so he couldn't steal them. Aneze didn't like to do it, but she would have to search another woman for her flint.

Aneze approached Tsedi's grandmother, who was crumpled up near the family fire pit. Grandmother was always the first one awake. She had probably been the only one awake when the enemies attacked. Her old ears must not have heard them coming. It wouldn't have taken more than a sharp blow to finish her off. In fact, Grandmother didn't seem much damaged at all. Even the animals hadn't touched her yet. Perhaps her flesh was too old to be tasty. Or perhaps it was her medicine that protected her.

Grandmother had very strong medicine, even though she was a woman. Women who knew hard times and suffered much could learn strong medicine. Grandmother's medicine was as strong as any hunters' medicine. Even great hunters with many wives and children asked Grandmother for help. They'd ask her to call out the animals, to make the fish swim into their traps, to cheat and destroy their enemies.

"Hush up! Silly children talk too much and never learn!" Mother had scolded Aneze and her brother one evening long ago. They were laughing at the way Grandmother fumbled with her cooking pots. She looked so frail, so clumsy. The old woman was pitiful.

"I will be happy if my children live to be as old as Grandmother," Mother told them. "She is stronger than you or I have proven yet to be. Don't laugh at her, help her," Mother urged. "Ask her to tell you stories. Maybe you'll learn something for a change."

So now Aneze tried to show respect as she approached the medicine woman's body. She also tried not to be afraid.

"Uh, excuse me, Grandmother." Aneze spoke out loud to make sure she could be heard. "Excuse me, but I must borrow your flint stone, Grandmother. My mother is gone, and I need to make fire."

Aneze waited for a moment. There seemed to be no objection. She found Grandmother's flint stone in the same place Mother hid hers, tied high up on the inside of her thigh. What kind of hiding place is it if everyone keeps their flint in the same spot? Aneze wondered. She tied the flint around her neck and hid it under her shirt instead.

"Thank you, Grandmother. I'll try to take good care of it," Aneze said.

AFTER THAT, ANEZE packed up a cooking pot. She put on the winter clothes she and Mother had just made up for her. She was too warm right now, but she would need them soon enough. She packed extra sinew ropes too. Like her winter clothes, they were made from Caribou. Now that she had no one to hunt the big animals for her, she wouldn't be able to make any more.

Aneze tied the bundle to her back. It was lighter than usual because she wasn't carrying all her brother's things. This was good because she had to move fast. She had decided where she was going. She was going to find Mother.

Girl

ANEZE FOLLOWED the trail all day.

The enemies were headed back to their own hunting grounds in the deep woods. She sweated under her furs. By the hottest part of the day, Aneze had to stop walking and stuff them into her bundle. She was tempted to leave them on the trail. What was she carrying them for? When she found her mother, the warriors would either kill her or adopt her. If they adopted her, her new father could give her skins for new clothes.

Aneze looked ahead. She could see the trail for some distance. It would be easy walking. She chewed on a piece of dried meat. What was she thinking? If she were allowed to join her mother and the group, she would be given to a husband, not a father. Aneze was almost big enough, after all, and they would insist she make herself useful. She shivered. Maybe she would hang on to her winter clothes for a while longer. She started walking again. She would have to keep moving if she was going to catch up with the others.

Aneze didn't want a new father anyway. Her real father had been good to her. He would never have forced her to be someone's wife if she didn't want to be. He gave her tongue and marrow to eat whenever he caught Caribou. They were the tastiest parts. They were supposed to be the hunter's portion.

"She's just a child, she doesn't know yet." Father always defended her.

Once Aneze had been pouring fresh water into the cooking pot. She wasn't being careful, and some of it ran into the fire that heated the stones.

"Ai-ai, so clumsy!" her mother cried out. Now the fire would have to be rebuilt. The stones sizzled with water. They would have to be heated up again. As if Mother didn't have enough to do, without having to do it twice.

"Wife." Father looked up from the ax-head he was making. "Dear Wife, let her be. She's just a child."

Mother didn't say anything. She looked hard at Aneze. Aneze got wood and rebuilt the fire herself. Nobody needed to tell her.

No, Aneze didn't want another father. But a husband would never say she was just a child. A husband would expect her to make the fire, heat the stones, boil the water, cook the meat, make the clothes, lie with him at night, look after the babies and carry all the things. Something inside Aneze seemed to rip open somewhere under her ribs. It made her catch her breath, this sudden hole. It felt wrong. It was as if she had always been full and now she was hollow. The hollow ached inside her as she walked.

Mother could carry many bundles all day and not become tired. She was tall and strong. If Aneze stumbled too much, Mother would carry her bundles for her as well. And Mother was good at sewing. Papa joked that skins wore out to dust before Mother's seams did. She had a good face too, nice to look at. She had an even color and no scars. Her teeth were strong and white. Father was proud of Mother. Even Aneze could figure that out.

Aneze was used to traveling all day. But she had never traveled all by herself. There was always Mother. Most times there were other wives and children too. And the hunters were never far, looking for animals to feed everyone. They were always together.

One autumn, their group was traveling to the barren ground to meet Caribou. They met a bigger group, also going to the great hunt. As was the custom, everyone sat down on the path. All was silent. Then Watonbee, the leader of the bigger group, spoke. "Much time has passed since we have seen each other. I tell you so that you may know the things that have befallen us all, hunters and wives.

"We mourn with Chewkoray, whose wife and baby were lost to the spring blizzard. We remember the courage of Tudantuay, gone in battle with Black Bear. We send death-songs to our old, our sick and our children, all taken last winter by the hunger."

Then Watonbee raised his head and cried out in clear ringing tones:

Dzeley, and her old mother too
Thalchini's son and daughter
Badelaye, weakened by lynx bite
and Benethatel, my own dear wife
I speak this death-song, so you hear my call
Ancestors, descendants, we remember them all

Everyone in Aneze's group hung their heads and wept when they heard of the people who had left them. Then, as was the custom, Father stood up and spoke for their group. He told the others all their sad news. Now the other group hung their heads, tore their hair and cried.

When this was finished, both groups stood up and mingled. Since all the sad business was known, there was only talk of good things. The children played games. There was laughter. Everyone was happy to be together again.

Aneze shifted the bundle on her back. She walked faster still. The group she was following had a full day's start on her. She didn't care what happened when she met them. She didn't want to be alone anymore. She couldn't wait to see Mother again.

"A hunter knows he is never alone." She had heard Father say that once.

Aneze looked into the trees. She spoke out loud to the bush. "There's always you, Chickadee," she said to the small birds skittering above. "And if I stare long enough at the sky, I'll see you, Eagle, circling with your wife. You will show me where Rabbit and Vole are hiding. And nearby in the stream, you are swimming, Jackfish. And you, Beaver, you are working on your house.

"You see," Aneze told the woods. "I'm not alone at all."

But that hollow inside told her something different. A hunter knows he is never alone. Father was a hunter, not Aneze. She was just a child.

Child

THEIR TRACK through the bush was easy to follow.

It was a well-worn path, but Aneze had never traveled it before. Was she in their territory now? She spotted the remains of a big camp—many fire pits. The warriors and their prisoners must have joined the wives and children. It suddenly occurred to Aneze that she should be more careful. She was tramping through the bush like Moose, maddened by blackflies. If she was tracking, she shouldn't disturb the bush. She should be watching, listening.

"The bush will tell you what you need to know," Father had explained to Brother.

Aneze knew some things. She knew that when a star falls it shows from which direction the wind will come tomorrow. She knew that a red sky just before sunrise means that lots of snow is coming by nightfall.

And when fog rests on the top of the hills—just the top—it means that warm weather is coming.

She looked around. She was in thick forest. Only sometimes did the sunlight reach her through the spruce and pine branches. She tried to make less sound on the forest floor. She crunched over the fallen needles and crackled small branches. It was hard to step lightly with a bundle on your back. But as Ancze grew quieter, she was able to hear more. She heard more than the cries of Chickadee and Wood Warbler. She could hear the rustle of creatures that did not want to be heard. Black Snake was twitching away, out of her path. And there was the sound of something scrambling for cover. Was it Porcupine?

Father would have known. Brother might have known. It was only she, who always stayed back at camp, who didn't know. Well, now she would try to know. That was all there was to it. She wasn't at camp now, was she? If she paid attention, maybe she could learn all the things Brother learned. All the things he used to learn.

"Brother, if only you could come back in a dream and teach me."

Without thinking, Aneze had spoken out loud. *Oops.* That was probably the first thing to learn. Keep your mouth shut.

"Keep your mouth shut or flies will get in." That was what her mother used to tell her when she was little. Aneze learned to help Mother with her mouth shut and her eyes open. If you were busy talking, how could you pay attention? How could you do the task yourself next time?

Aneze walked much farther. The tracks brought her close to a small creek. She drank. As she raised her head, she smelled it. Meat. Cooked meat. She found a small piece, dropped in the dust and forgotten. Probably by a child. Aneze sat very still. She listened hard, but she couldn't hear anything. The group must have moved on already.

Farther down the creek she found another camp. It was big, like the first one. They had left behind the remains of two caribou. They hadn't dried the leftovers. That would have meant staying in place, waiting another day or two. They must want to keep moving.

Aneze gave a low whistle of regret. If they had stayed to dry the meat, she might be with Mother now. There was no time to lose. Without even scavenging any food from the bones, Aneze retied her bundle and slung it onto her back. If she hurried, she might catch up with them by nightfall. Aneze ran after them. She forgot that she wasn't supposed to make noise.

THEN, QUITE SUDDENLY, Aneze found Mother. She was running so fast she almost missed her. But Aneze recognized her, even crumpled up like that, with her hair all over her face. They'd thrown her into the bush, a little ways off the trail.

"Mama?" Aneze whispered. She approached slowly. It was too horrible to think about. Aneze's heart was pounding too loud. She tripped over a branch.

"Mama, wake up, it's me. I came after you."

Mother didn't move. Mother didn't even breathe.

Aneze knew it. She knew it as soon as she saw the body. It was just taking a while to hit her. She wanted to talk to Mother again.

She rolled the body over. She smoothed the hair from the face. Someone had cut Mother's throat. There was a red and black bruise across her beautiful cheek. She looked strange. She had Mother's face, but she didn't quite look like Mama anymore.

"Aaaaaiiiiieee…" The smallest sound in the world came out of Aneze. She rocked on her heels over the body.

"Aiiii…maaaamaaaaa…," Aneze squeaked. Mama's beautiful face was getting wet. "Maaaamaaaa…don't leave meeeee…"

Aneze felt herself getting smaller and smaller. Soon her mother would be as big as a tree. Then Aneze would

crawl inside Mother's flint pocket and stay there.
"Maaaamaaaa, everybody left me. I'm all by myself—
and I'm just a child, Mama! I'm too little to be
alone…Maaamaa."

Aneze curled up next to her mother. She put her
head on Mother's shoulder and wrapped Mother's arm
around her. She wasn't warm, but she still smelled like
Mother.

Finally the black came back.

Boy

WHEN ANEZE woke up, the light was already leaving the sky.

She shivered. Up close like this, she could see the knife slash on Mother's neck. Which of them did this? She'd kill them for it. She'd kill them all. She'd stab them too. First in the legs, so they couldn't run. Then in the arms, so they couldn't fight. Then in the stomach— she'd leave her knife in there and they could just twist and scream and die slowly like that.

And she had been trying to join them! How weak. What had she been thinking? They had killed Father and Brother. Mother had refused to stay with them— look at her! Someone had lost his temper on her. She must have been giving them a lot of trouble.

"*AAAHHHHHH*!" Aneze sat up and shouted as loud as she could.

She hoped they heard her; she'd fight them all. The hollow inside her grew bigger. It filled her up. She was a big black hole. Aneze was gone. On the sound of her cries, Aneze was being carried out to that first evening star. "*AAAAHHHHH…!*"

Aneze laid her head down on Mother and sobbed. Everyone had gone. And she was still here—how could it be? She was still here…just a big empty hole.

But she *was* still here. Just like the trees and the birds and the frogs and the flies. Everything was quiet after all that shouting and crying. But they were still here, all of them.

Aneze had been stupid to think Mother would accept a new family. Not that way. Mother was content to be with Father. What about the time another hunter had wanted Mother for his wife? Aneze should have remembered that time on the trail with Watonbee and his people.

"I'm thinking that I have need of another wife. What will you take for yours?" Watonbee had asked Aneze's father. Watonbee had been admiring Mother for some time. Mother had told Father about the hunter's glances.

Watonbee was a great hunter. He led many families to the barren ground, following Caribou. His household was large, with seven wives and many children. He knew the land and the weather and the animals. He could provide for all those wives and children. He was wise enough to keep order among them. It was natural that he should lead other families too. Father had to be careful not to offend such an important man.

"You have so many wives," Father had replied. "I'm not special. I have only one. Don't take a man's only wife. Let her stay with me. Let me keep my children. There are many good daughters among us who need a strong husband like you. Any hunter would be honored to give you a wife from his family."

Watonbee nodded his head and rose from Father's fire. The hunters who came with him rose too.

"Any hunter would be honored," Watonbee said, "except one." As he left, he turned around.

"I'll wrestle you for her tomorrow, at first light," he said.

The other hunters laughed.

"Better get some sleep," Watonbee said.

That night, Aneze had lain awake under the furs. Her feet were right by the fire, but she couldn't get warm. In the darkness, Mother wailed. Mother didn't want to go with Watonbee. She was content to be with Father. And she didn't want to share a husband with many wives. Everyone knew that Father could take care of more women and children if he wanted to. But he didn't, because he knew Mother didn't like to share.

Aneze heard Father murmuring to Mother. She couldn't hear what he said, but she heard Mother's reply. "And what if you do win?" Mother wept. "Watonbee will never let you walk away from that. He'll be very angry. People will laugh and say he's getting old and weak."

Aneze heard her father's low rumble again. Mother had kept on sobbing, but more quietly this time.

Aneze looked at Mother's body now. Aneze would bet those enemies never saw her crying. Not even when they punched her face.

What was the use in remembering all this about Mother and Father? She didn't like it. It made the hollow inside her grow bigger. Aneze should forget that she ever had a family.

But she couldn't help it. She remembered what had happened that next morning, at first light.

Watonbee was pacing back and forth outside her family's tent.

"What's taking you so long?" he called. "Afraid to come out?"

Everyone had gathered around, of course. A wrestling match was good entertainment. Word had spread quickly around the camp the night before. Everyone wanted to see what was going to happen.

Aneze could hear them all laughing at what Watonbee said.

"It must be hard to leave your wife's side this cold morning!" he joked for the crowd. "Especially since it is for the last time!"

Inside the tent, Mother was working quickly on the last bit of Father's back. Sometime during the night, Father had cut off all his hair. Now Mother was covering him in bear grease. When every part of his body was completely slick and shiny, Father rushed out of the tent. The whole family tumbled out right behind him.

They were in time to see Father give Watonbee a surprise head-butt. He plowed the taller man right over into the dirt. The crowd laughed. This was not strictly fair wrestling, but it sure was funny to see. Watonbee jumped up and grabbed Father's ears to pull him to the ground. But his hands slid right off Father because of the bear grease. That was even funnier. So was the surprised expression on Watonbee's face. Aneze laughed along with everyone else.

Then she felt herself being tugged back into the tent. It was Mother.

"Get packing," she told Aneze and her brother. She threw bundles at them. "We're leaving." They did as they were told. Outside the tent, another burst of laughter could be heard. Watonbee was shouting. He sounded mad.

"Hurry, hurry," Mother urged.

"I'm just getting the cooking pot," Aneze said.

Since the cooking pot was outside, this meant Aneze got to sneak a quick look before she had to rush in again. Father was clowning around a little, acting like a fool. People were laughing. Watonbee was on the ground, trying to scrape grease off his palms.

"It looks like the match is over, Ma," Aneze announced as she came in through the tent flap.

"We'll leave as soon as your father puts his clothes back on. Let's give Watonbee a chance to calm his temper without having to see our faces."

The family made as little fuss as possible when they left. They nodded their good-byes to friends and relatives. This year they would not be joining everyone on the barren ground to meet Caribou, that's all. It couldn't be helped. Out of respect for Watonbee, they would keep away for a season. After that it should all be blown over. Watonbee had retired to his tent. His wives were tending his scratches.

Aneze was sad to be leaving the big group. It would be a while before she got to play with her friends again. She followed Father's bare head as he cut a trail for them. He didn't look like Father with his hair cut off.

"Didn't Father think he could beat Watonbee fair and square, without the bear grease?" she asked her brother.

"Don't be stupid," Brother snapped. "Of course he could. Father had to make a joke out of it—out of himself.

How else could he keep us all together without starting some kind of war with Watonbee and his people?"

It was a good thing Aneze had Brother to explain things to her. It was a good thing Father was so clever at keeping Mother.

Except now Aneze was alone.

Even so, she had been wrong to follow the wife stealers. That was a mistake. She understood that now. She combed out her mother's hair with her fingers. Aneze wanted to lie down again. She wanted to lie down and never get up. Fallen branches would cover her. Then snow would come. Timid animals would come out, curious. She would open her eyes and stare. Nothing would make her get up. She wouldn't, even if Bear ate her foot. Even if Eagle ate her eyes, she would keep staring. She wished she had dug out that enemy's eye when she'd had the chance. If only she had known what he was going to do to her...to her family.

She would have pulled out his eyes and crunched them between her teeth so he could never make war again, never shoot an arrow straight. He could never feed his family, and they would all starve and die. See how *they* liked it.

Aneze let go of her mother's hair and let out a great war whoop, like Brother and his friends used to do. "*AHHWAAHHHHH*! *AYAYAYAYAY Aiiiiie*!"

Birds fluttered out of the trees, offended by the noise. Aneze stood up and stomped around. "*YAH*! *YAH* ! *WAHHHHH*!"

She wasn't going to lie down. It wasn't going to be that easy.

Aneze pulled out her knife and started cutting off her hair. She would fight smart, like Father. Great ropes of hair fell around her. It hurt; the knife pulled a lot. She would just have to learn to bear it. She would just have to learn.

Aneze gathered all her hair and made a cushion for Mother's head. Then Aneze scratched at the bloodstained earth under Mother. It was wet. She used it to paint her face, to make herself look scary, like a warrior. There.

She untied Mother's flint pocket and put it with her own. She removed Mother's leggings. Aneze's leggings were wearing thin. She smoothed Mother's tunic down. She had to get going, out of this territory. She didn't want to run into enemies right now.

She'd go north, straight to the barren ground, far away. Aneze was sick of this forest anyway.

Orphan

THE NIGHTS were longer now.

Aneze traveled slowly. She knew it was important to catch all the food she could. She set traps and doubled back to check them. If she was lucky, her traps caught rabbits. It always took a while to dry any extra meat and the skins. But she needed the meat for the times her traps stayed empty. And those skins would be useful as it got colder.

One day, Aneze stopped to camp near a small river. She set up a lean-to, using sticks and bushy branches. She placed her bundle behind it. Then she walked some distance away, along the water. She kept very quiet. She wanted to catch frogs. She could hear them singing. Frogs made a good meal. Their skin popped as they roasted. Then she heard something else, a great splash in deep water. Aneze checked the direction of the breeze.

She crept nearer. She peered through the branches.

It was Beaver. He was working on his house, making it sturdy. It was piled high with tree branches. He had chewed them with his long front teeth. His house was stuck together with river mud and clay that he scooped up with his broad tail. In this house, he and his family would huddle and stay warm. When the river froze over, they would be safe under the solid ice all winter long.

But just look at him! He was very fat, and his coat was so thick and glossy. What if Aneze could catch Beaver? That would be a lot of food! And the pelt would be much better than her rabbit skins.

Aneze crept back to her camp. She had two knives now: her brother's and one she had found in Mother's pocket. She could spare one of these and tie it on a stick to make a spear. She found a strong straight branch and cut away all the brush. She cut a notch into one end. She fit the knife handle into the notch and wrapped it tight onto the branch with a thong, around and around. That ought to hold firm, she hoped.

She balanced the spear lightly in one hand. How much did the knife's weight pull it down? When she threw it, how would it fly? Oh, why hadn't she paid more attention to the spears that Father and Brother made?

She crept back to the river to spy on Beaver. He was swimming from his house to the shore. He must want more branches. This was a bit of luck. Aneze waited until Beaver waddled up onto the riverbank. She begged the wind not to shift direction. Beaver mustn't find out she was watching.

Aneze hadn't thrown a spear in a long while. When she was little, her brother had shown her how as a joke. Now she wished she had time for some practice throws.

She waited until Beaver was high up on the bank but not yet hidden by the trees. Now she must throw—now! The spear whizzed straight. That was what Father called first-time luck. But how was her aim? Would it strike?

Thunk! The knifepoint landed on Beaver's wide tail. He screamed and pulled away, ripping his tail down the middle. Aneze jumped out of the bush and scrambled toward Beaver, her other knife ready. Beaver's surprise and terror made him freeze for a split second before he freed himself from the spear that pinned his tail. That one second was enough. Aneze threw her whole weight on him. Before he could fight her off, she stabbed him through the ribs.

Beaver's panic gave him the strength of ten. He thrashed under Aneze. He tried to shake her off.

He gnashed his teeth and swiped his claws. Aneze panicked too. Why wouldn't he die? She had to kill him now; she'd hurt him too much. She stabbed at the writhing body, over and over. Would he ever stop thrashing? What a mess!

Finally, Beaver stopped moving. Aneze sat on the bank, panting. She was covered in Beaver's blood and some of her own too. Any real hunter would be ashamed of such a kill. Had she ruined the pelt? She couldn't stop shaking. If only she had better aim. She should kill quickly, calmly. Beaver was no Rabbit, that was certain.

She picked up the spear. She would have to practice. She stood up and sang a death-song to Beaver, the way a hunter was supposed to. She didn't know if there were special words. But Aneze was sure Beaver would know what she meant.

"I thank you, Beaver, for giving your life to this very poor, unskilled hunter. You were a strong opponent and I honor you."

There, that sounded like a pretty good death-song.

On second thought, she added, "I'm sorry I stabbed you so much. I really didn't mean any disrespect by it."

Then she leaned down and picked Beaver up by the base of his tail. With her spear over her shoulder and her prey hanging by her side, Aneze headed back to the lean-to. It was time to make a fire and then skin and gut Beaver. For a moment, Aneze felt like a real hunter.

SNOW COVERED THE ground now. Aneze wore her winter clothes all the time. She made herself snowshoes out of branches. She tied them to her feet with sinew. They were a bit messy, but Aneze thought they were pretty good. They kept her on top of the snowdrifts. Otherwise, she would sink up to her knees with every step.

The land was changing. She had been walking for a long time. The trees were smaller. There were wide-open spaces now, between the trees. The wind blew through them—blew hard. It was very cold. Aneze had never been to this land when it was so cold. Her family had always returned to the forest by now. Her snowshoes crunched on the ground. *Crunch, crunch, crunch*. She tried to keep a nice even beat. *Crunch, crunch, crunch*. Inside her head, she made up a song to go with the sound.

Where do you go?
I don't know
What do you think you will find there?
I carry a sack
Upon my back
And I will leave it behind there

Aneze liked her song, even if it didn't make any sense. It was a traveling song. It helped to carry her farther and farther along. She'd stopped looking for animals. It seemed too much trouble to hunt now. She hadn't found anything fresh to eat for a while. Her dried meat was almost gone. She had been careful not to be greedy, to make it last. But she had only a little bit left. Soon she would start on her clothes. She would tear off a small piece, where she could spare it. She would chew on that. That's what her family always did when the animals refused to be caught.

Aneze kept walking north. She knew it was a silly thing to do. At first it had been a good idea. If she met Caribou, she just might meet other people hunting too. Maybe they would help her, give her meat and skins in exchange for her help sewing skins. But she hadn't found Caribou. She didn't know how. Usually everyone followed an older person, someone who had an idea about where to find Caribou. Aneze didn't know how they knew, but much of the time they were right.

But by this time both Caribou and people were back in the trees. Caribou could eat the lichen off the tree trunks all winter long, no matter how deeply the snow covered the plants on the ground. So why was Aneze walking in the other direction, toward nothing but ice? The ice was too thick to fish through. But her snowshoes didn't turn around. *Crunch, crunch, crunch*. She had no tent and no tent poles. *Crunch, crunch, crunch*.

> *I carry a sack*
> *Upon my back*
> *And I will leave it behind me*

Now Aneze was sure of it —she had gone a little crazy. She had been wandering alone for too long. She remembered a story about a hunter who wandered and wandered in search of his dream-vision. But his dream-vision never came to him, and he stopped caring about anything. He didn't bother hunting anymore; he didn't eat. Aneze considered stopping to gather some scrubby branches. She could use them to make a fire, later on. But the snowshoes rocked her from side to side, and she kept walking. She wasn't going to stop.

Later still, when the moon was full in the sky, Aneze kept walking, walking. She had no idea how far she walked. She left the trees far behind. Now she could see forever in every direction. Except that there was nothing to see…It was different from the forest. It was beautiful, but in a scary way. It was dark, but the snow gave some light. The wind was terrible. It gusted against her and tried to blow her off her snowshoes. Whenever she grew too tired, Aneze dug a hole in the snow. She sat in it, just to let the wind blow over her head for a while. When the wind died down a little, she climbed out and started walking again.

Then, one time, she didn't want to climb out of the hole.

I don't want to walk anymore, she thought. I'm too cold. I'm too skinny to do this any longer. Aneze made some effort to warm herself. She sat on the beaver pelt. She rested her back against the bundle. But her heart wasn't really in it. Her heart was somewhere else. Her heart didn't really believe any of it mattered.

So this is where you walked, was Aneze's last thought before her mind went to join her heart.

Ahwak

SHE FELT warm.

She was hot! It burned!

Aneze cried out. Her cheeks were on fire. She reached up to put out the fire, but someone held her hand back.

"Don't touch. You'll rub your skin off. Let it heal."

Aneze's ears felt a bit creaky. It had been a long time since she had heard another voice. She tried to pay attention. There was no wind. It was warm. Over there was a glowing light—a small fire. Next to the fire sat a small man. He looked old—older than Father. But there was no one else. No wife, no children in the tent. But was it a tent? Aneze reached out to touch the side. It was snow. She was in a tent made of snow!

"Here, drink this." The old man gave her a bowl.

Steam rose off the top. "You need some food. You really are pitiful." This strange man spoke the language of her people. How could it be? Maybe he knew magic. That would explain the fire and the hot soup in the snow. How had he found her? What did he plan to do with her?

His soup was good. It tasted peculiar. He cooked a strange meat. More magic possibly. But the soup was hot and rich. She could already feel her strength coming back.

"Don't touch your face," the old man told her. Aneze hadn't noticed, but her hand was reaching up to her cheek again. It hurt.

"The cold has eaten you," the old man explained. "You have given some skin to the wind. But not too much. I checked your fingers and toes. You'll keep those. You are strong. Nobody cares for you, yet you are still alive. Why do you have no hunter to look after you?"

Aneze sat up a little straighter. She had spent all that time in the woods, alone. She had looked after herself. She had killed Beaver.

"I am a hunter!" she told him.

The old man stopped drinking his soup. He gazed at her for some time. His eyes hid deep inside his face.

What was he looking at? Was he going to laugh at her? She was so pitiful, after all; he said it himself.

Nobody could believe she was a hunter. Maybe he was deciding to curse her as a liar and send her back into the cold. Or maybe he was making a spell that would turn her into soup for his pot. Aneze tried very hard to keep her face still, her eyes steady. A hunter can keep his thoughts to himself.

"Well then, hunter," he said at last. He took a sip from his bowl. "What brings you so far from your hunting grounds, if I may ask?"

"My people died," was all Aneze said.

He nodded. "If your people leave you, then it is good to try something new."

Aneze took another drink of soup. Everything here was certainly new.

"If you like, you may stay with me for a while. I am alone much of the time. It might be nice to have the company of another, ah, hunter." The old man smiled a little over his soup bowl. "What can I call you, besides hunter?"

Aneze searched for a name, a hunter's name. One who was brave and strong. One who wasn't afraid, not even of making war. She remembered her war cry, back in the forest.

"*Ahh…wah*, Ahwah. You can call me Ahwah," she told the old man.

"Ahwak. Well then." He shrugged. "Orphan Ahwak,

I travel between my people. I bring them news. I visit. They like that. You can travel with me if you like."

A small sigh escaped from Aneze—she must have been holding her breath. She sank deeper under the furs. She looked around the magical tent of snow, made warm by a fire that burned without wood or smoke. The old man had rescued her—a poor orphan without people. That meant he must be kind, didn't it? She thought she might like to stay a while. She thought she might like that very much.

AT FIRST ANEZE couldn't figure it out. Everything was so different. Then she decided that the old man must have used his powers to transport her to another world. It was a very strange world. Most astonishing, there was not a single tree in the whole land. The old man assured Aneze that water and earth and rocks lay under the snow, but it was difficult to imagine. Sometimes Aneze could see so far that it looked like the ground and the sky were one. Sometimes the winds and snow blocked her view of her own feet. And then there were the dogs. The old man lived with so many.

"I need my dogs," the old man told her. "They pull my sled."

He spoke to these dogs in a strange dog-language.

And they listened. They did what he asked them to do. He taught her some of the dog-language so that when she spoke to them, they listened to her too.

Even the cold air was magic, in a fierce way. Often they ran alongside the sled while the dogs pulled. It helped to keep everyone warm when they traveled. But one of these times, Aneze felt water pouring down her face. Not from her eyes, but from her nose. How odd. She turned to the old man, running on the other side of the sled. He was wounded! There was blood pouring from his nose! Aneze cried out. He looked over to her.

"Get back on the sled!" he ordered. "We'll stop soon and make a snow house!"

It was too cold to travel, he told her later. The air was so angry it was cutting their insides, making them bleed. They would drink hot snow-water and wait for the air to warm up outside.

When they stopped to rest, the old man showed Aneze how to make a snow house. The dogs always slept outside in the wind. It must be the magic that made them so strong. The old man showed Aneze how to find the good snow with his finding stick. The good snow lay hidden under the soft snow. When they found it, they scooped away the soft snow to make a circle shape, just big enough for two. She watched the old man, and she learned everything she could. She saw how to cut blocks from the good snow. She saw how they could be cut to fit around the edge of the circle they cleared. She wasn't very good at it. But she was able to pack extra snow into the cracks. This made smooth walls that kept the winds out.

There was always something for her to do. In the snow house, she learned how to keep the small fire burning on the fire stone. She learned that the magic burning water on the stone was not water at all. It was the fat part of Seal, the animal the old man hunted. Seal was the most magic thing of all. What a strange animal Seal was! He lived in the water, under the ice. But he was not a fish. He breathed air and he had fur, but he had a tail like a fish.

Aneze smiled to herself when she thought of the first time she had watched the old man prepare Seal for them to eat. He had dragged the furry body onto a clean piece of ice. He crouched down and sliced open the belly. He pulled out a flap of red, soggy, dripping flesh. Then he leaned over and gobbled it up! Just like that! No boiling, no roasting, no nothing. Aneze backed away a few steps. He was acting like a wild animal.

The old man looked over at her and laughed. He washed his fingers in the snow and started to skin Seal.

"Later, I'll give you some to try," he told her, grinning at the look on her face. "You'll love it. It's the most delicious part, the hunter's part."

That first time seemed so far away now. Aneze had long since learned to eat the hunter's part. She got used to it.

"Delicious, right?" The old man nodded and hummed whenever they ate that first bloody meal off their fresh-caught meat.

"Uhmm-mmm!" Aneze would nod and hum back in agreement. Actually she preferred the soup they made later. But she didn't ever tell the old man that.

It certainly was the most peculiar world. Aneze was lucky to be protected by the old man's power. The cold and the snow were his tools. They were just waiting for him to put them to use.

The old man gave her a suit of his clothes. He gave her a soft shirt and trousers, as well as a parka, mittens and short outer-trousers that dropped down to the edge of a pair of high boots. He was no taller than she was, only wider and sturdier. Inside these new clothes, she never froze. She wore socks with the fur side in. Her boots had the fur side out. She wore the inner set of clothing in the snow house, to feed the dogs and to do other work around camp. When they traveled and when they hunted, she wore the outer clothes on top.

It was always dark in this world. The sun showed for a little while, low and pale. It must be very tired, trying to warm the snow that never left. It rested on the ground before it sank away again.

The old man taught Aneze how to catch Seal through the ice. First, the dogs found a breathing hole under the snow. They got very excited. They jumped around and wagged their tails. Then the old man led them away from the hole. No seal would ever come to a hole with all that racket.

Next, the old man dug through the soft snow to the thin dome of ice that grew over the breathing hole. He carefully cracked through that. Then he sent down his searcher stick. This told him which way the breathing tunnel went—all the way through the ice down to the sea. Now that the old man understood the tunnel, he could drive his harpoon through it, straight into Seal.

But Seal would never come to a dead hole, a hole that had been broken through. So while Aneze set up the harpoon rest, the old man placed his snow-finding stick in the breathing hole. This held a small airhole clear as he piled snow back over the breathing hole. When a fresh mound of snow covered the breathing hole once more, the old man eased the stick out. This left a very small tunnel through the snow, straight to the breathing hole. He placed a fluffy down feather over the top. He used his spit to stick it to a tiny bird claw. The claw held the feather onto the snow. Around all this he placed a small fence made of sealskin. The ends were attached to make a circle that would keep wind away. Not even the lightest puff should disturb the feather.

The old man placed his harpoon on its rest by the hole. He and Aneze stood on his furry toolbag. This kept their feet warmer. They waited for a very long time. They watched the feather.

Aneze knew that she shouldn't move.

She knew that she had better not speak.

What a long time it took. They had to wait for Seal to come to the hole.

One time, Aneze got too cold just standing there —so still, so long. She didn't want to be like the dogs, though. They weren't allowed to hunt by the hole. They couldn't be trusted to keep quiet. The wind was strong that day. It seemed to be blowing harder than before. Inside the sealskin fence, the feather remained still. Aneze huddled deeper into her hood. Would Seal ever come? The old man was like a stone. They had been watching this stupid feather forever. It was his magic, no doubt, that made him able to do this kind of hunting. But she was just a child! She couldn't stand it much more. She was going to have to run, jump, bark, shout—do something—pretty soon. She could creep off and go play with the dogs. She would have to leave quietly, or the old man would be so angry with her. She would do it…any time now. All right, this time she was really going to leave…*riiigght now…riigh…t…*

The feather moved!

Its little fluffy strands lifted up—air! Air was coming up though the breathing hole!

The old man's harpoon sliced through the snow mound, down through the tunnel in the ice. The sharp harpoon head lodged in the animal below. The harpoon head was only loosely attached to the stick, so it would break away and stay with Seal. The old man pulled out the stick. He hung on to the line that was tied tightly to the harpoon head. Seal and the old man pulled this way and that, each on his own side of the ice. Seal struggled, but the old man was too strong. Aneze helped to dig out the breathing hole and pull up the body. Beautiful, fat, glistening Seal! In no time, they had slit open the belly. They ate the steaming insides.

Then they brought the sled around and loaded up the body. The smell of blood made the dogs crazy. They were hungry too. But the old man turned them toward camp. They could eat leftovers after they had done their job. The old man flicked his whip, just to show them he meant it.

Aneze and the old man ran alongside the sled. Aneze felt the creaky frost leave her legs and arms. This was good, because back at camp there was much work to be done.

Hunting Partners

INSIDE THE snow house, it was easy to forget the cold outside.

Aneze gave the fire more fat. It burned warmer. The old man was feeding the dogs outside. He kept them tied up, far apart, whenever they ate.

"One time I forgot," he had told Aneze. "They were snapping at that meat so fast, one of them ate the lead dog's tongue. Poor dog didn't know what hit him. He just stood there, mouth open, closed, open, closed. Couldn't find his tongue! I had to kill him. Now I remember to keep them tied up and separate."

Aneze had shut her mouth tight and wiggled her tongue around. It was in there, safe and sound. She knew that.

The old man came inside and sat on the sleeping platform. His feet stuck straight out. They stayed warmer that way than if they touched the ground.

"Some soup would be nice," he said.

Aneze poured soup into a bowl and passed it over.
Now they were warm. The rest of the seal meat lay
bundled out on the porch, safe from the dogs and other
animals. It was probably freezing up already. Everything
was just as it should be. There was nothing more to do
but rest and sleep.

It was only then that Aneze remembered the hollow
inside her, behind her rib. It was odd how she never felt
it when they were hunting. She only noticed it when
work was done and her belly was full. Maybe it was
chased away by the cold. She wondered if the old man
ever missed his family.

"Where is your family?" Aneze asked him. *Oops.*
What a nosy question. It was none of her business. She
knew better than that. But the old man's shiny face just
wrinkled into a smile.

"I have family all over. I took a wife three times, but I
outlived them all. I'm too strong, I guess." He shrugged.
"I have relatives in every winter camp. But I only like to
visit for a little while. I'm old, but I'm not tired yet. I can
still chew meat and drink soup!" He raised his empty
bowl high. Then he put it down on the clean snow floor.

"I can even mend boots!" he exclaimed as he pulled
out a bone shard and a length of sinew thread from
his pack.

"Scoot over here, Ahwak," he ordered. "A hunter must know how to mend boots if he travels with no wife." He stopped his work. His eyes widened as he looked up. "You don't have a wife hidden on you somewhere, do you?"

What a joker.

"In that case, you'd better pay attention to what I'm doing. Your feet will never be wet."

Aneze tried to copy the tiny stitches the old man made. He certainly had a lot of powers. His stitches were even smaller than Mother's!

THE LONG NIGHTS went on forever in this world. Through it all, Aneze watched and copied the old man. She got used to waiting for Seal. Her stitches got smaller. Soon she was cutting blocks for their snow houses. Sometimes she was allowed to cut up the seals they caught. But the old man always skinned them himself. He always sewed up the hole his harpoon made. Of course he was the one who decided where they would go to look for more animals for their food and fire. He didn't get it right every time, so they had to spend most of their time hunting, just to get enough.

"There are so many breathing holes for Seal to use," Aneze said one time. "How do you know which one he will visit?"

"I don't," the old man replied. "I choose a good hole, a nice hole. Then I stand by it, and I ask Seal to please come to me. What else can I do? If Seal is willing, then he will come. If my sons were with me, we could stand over many holes at once."

He paused. Then he said, "But since I have only young Hunter Ahwak, I have to ask extra nice." His eyes disappeared into his smile. He pushed Aneze. She laughed as she struggled to stay standing.

"I wish I could talk to the animals, like you." Aneze sighed. "Like the dog-language you speak, so they understand."

"That's not dog-language!" the old man exclaimed. Then he started speaking a long stream of dog-language, right there. She'd never heard him speak so much in dog-language. Her mouth dropped.

"This is not dog-language! This is the language of my people, you little forest-fool!" He laughed. "Hand me that line, would you? This sled needs tying." He shook his head as he tied the slat down firmly so it wouldn't wiggle anymore. "The little hunter thinks I speak dog," he murmured to himself.

"There was a time, you know…" He looked up from his work for a moment. "There was a time when people and animals spoke the same language. Did your parents ever tell you that?"

Aneze nodded. She had heard a lot of stories.

"But now, mostly we just have to listen. It's not so easy anymore." He finished with the sled and gathered up the harpoon heads. He handed one to Aneze for sharpening. They could go inside now.

"My dogs, they listen hard to me because I feed them and I raised them. But the animals, they feed us, don't they? We have to do the begging and the listening."

They crawled in through the porch and into the main room of the snow house.

"That goes for the snow too." He gestured around at the walls and the ceiling. "It covers us, doesn't it? I have to listen to the weather if I want the snow to take care of me, don't I?"

Aneze nodded. It was the same with her people. Everyone listened to the weather. And when the elders spoke, people listened. That was because the elders had learned things, because they knew.

"It takes practice," the old man said. "We must do it over and over. Like that harpoon head you grind. If you grind it over and over, it will be sharp and do its job well." He held up the harpoon head he was working on. It was so sharp she could almost see the firelight through the edge. He passed it to her. She would make hers sharp like this.

"Maybe you can catch Seal next time, Hunter Ahwak."

Aneze nodded. She was going to listen, and she was going to practice. She was going to live a very long time. The old man tamped out some of the fire. Now it was low. It was time to get some sleep.

Funny, the hollow didn't bother her so much now.

Breakup

EVERYTHING WAS changing in the old man's world.

The old man didn't seem worried, so Aneze thought it must be all right. The sun visited the world longer and longer each day. It rose higher in the sky, just like in her own world. This meant that spring and summer were coming. It had been impossible to imagine this world without snow and ice, but now they were melting away. The sled did not move so well now. The dogs had to work very hard to pull it. Sometimes Aneze and the old man would pull too.

"Soon we will take this sled apart, when it becomes too much trouble to pull," he told her.

The ground was cracking. Seals came out of the cracks and sunned themselves. Hunting was easier— wetter, but easier.

"Breakup," the old man said. "Breakup is coming.

All this—" he gestured at the ice beneath their feet, "all this will be water soon."

These days the old man kept a sharp eye on the ice beneath their feet, because you never knew.

CRAAACK! *KA-BAM*! *BOOOM*! *GRUMBLE*! *ROAR*!

The ice made sounds like lightning and thunder. Terrible sounds. And then the ground would rise up, up, up. A great mountain of ice could rise up where it was flat before. Aneze worried that one of these mountains would rise up under them. What if she got stuck alone on one side of the mountain with the old man on the other. She stayed close by him now. She never wandered.

"We must get off the sea. It is time to go to the caribou crossing," the old man said. "There you will meet the others. We'll hunt Caribou together, hunting partner."

Caribou! It had been so long since Aneze had tasted Caribou!

"Yes." The old man smacked his lips. "It'll be good to eat caribou fat for a change!"

IT WAS A long journey. The sled runners turned to mush. The ice layers that kept them smooth just wouldn't stay frozen anymore. They clogged up with the stones and grasses that were peeking out from the snow. Aneze wore a different suit of clothes now. It was made of sealskin. The old man had pulled it out from among the old clothes they kept on the sleeping platform.

"That should keep the water off you," he told her as he changed into his own suit.

As the world changed, so did the old man. He whistled more often. He sang songs in his own language. He talked more.

"Ha, I wonder if Alareak managed to find Polar Bear this winter. He swore his wife would eat bear meat." He turned to Aneze. "Alareak's wife likes to eat bear meat when she has a child in her belly." Then he turned away again. "I wonder if she had a boy or a girl." He was always talking to himself these days. "Kapuuq will have hunted his first seal already. I mustn't forget to tease him about it. I'll tell him Seal is easy. Walrus—now that's a real hunter's animal, heh, heh."

Aneze worried about this. What if the old man got tired of her with all his family around? What if the others weren't kind, like him? They might drive her off. Or worse, they might want to kill her. After all, she was a stranger. What's more, she was an orphan. She hoped the old man would defend her. Just in case, she found her knife in her pack and kept it close by.

And then suddenly, one day, they arrived. They walked over the crest of a hill, and before them was a wide river. The water flowed. The ice was almost gone. On the next hill she could see skin tents and people moving about. Aneze could see a group of children playing off by the rocks. She could see women going in and out of their tents. The hollow inside her jumped. It had been a long time since Aneze had been with many people.

"Come on, come on!" the old man urged Aneze and the dogs. "Hai! Hai!" He shouted and waved. Then he took off. Aneze and the dogs followed.

"Hai! Hai!" Aneze heard the response from the next crest. "Idloq is here!"

Aneze saw them swarming toward her, short and broad in their peculiar skin clothes. For a moment, she forgot that she was wearing the same clothes. They crowded around her. She wasn't used to them. They smelled different.

"Idloq, we've been eating fish!"

"Idloq, come by my fire. I've made tea!"

"Have you heard, Uncle, have you heard? Papa says Caribou are coming!"

They were hard to understand. They talked too fast and used many words Aneze had not learned.

They crowded very close. One woman drew the old man away with her. Aneze made sure to stick to him like spruce sap. She wasn't going to be left alone with these strangers.

Everything was quieter by the woman's fire. The day was so fine, she kept her stone lamp outside. They crouched near it and received the bowl of tea she offered. She wore a very fine suit of black and white caribou skin. She had sewn the pieces into a beautiful pattern. When she turned, Aneze saw that she kept a baby in her hood. Now wasn't that clever!

Whenever the woman spoke to the old man, she kept her eyes low. The funny thing was the old man never looked directly at the woman either. Even when he took the cup of tea from her, he looked away. It was not like when Aneze and the old man had their chats by the fire. The woman cast some sharp glances over to Aneze, but she didn't say anything. Nobody said anything. That came later, when the men came back.

Everyone shared the meal together. The women and children sat in one circle. The men and the older boys sat together. Aneze sat next to the old man. She kept her head down and ate her soup—fish! That was a nice change. Everyone was chatting. The mood seemed friendly enough. Then she heard a loud comment. She wasn't sure, but she thought she understood.

"What's this long weed you've brought among us, Idloq?"

Aneze looked up. One of the hunters pushed his chin in Aneze's direction. He was looking at the old man. Everyone else continued eating. But the talking stopped. All ears were wide open.

"Long weed"? Had he called her a "long weed"? Aneze was quite sure she'd understood that much. His expression wasn't friendly.

"This is Ahwak, Orphan Ahwak," the old man said quietly. A few stopped eating to hear him better. "I found him in the snow. He was my hunting partner this winter."

The unfriendly hunter said something Aneze couldn't catch.

"Sure he's a hunter," the old man replied. "Maybe he looks like a girl because he's young. His beard hasn't grown in, that's all. He's from the forest, you know. They look different. Look how tall he is."

How astonishing! How come she understood the old man so well? It was as if he was speaking in her own language! And yet the others acted like they heard nothing strange. Could he be speaking both languages at once? She knew it; he *was* magic! She turned to him. He was looking at her out of the side of one eye. It winked.

It was too strange. She put her face back over her soup bowl. Luckily, that seemed to be the end of that. Nobody else bothered Aneze after that. They didn't even give her funny looks. When they found out that she could speak only a few words of their language, they didn't talk to her much either.

After eating they went to see the kayaks. The old man's sons had hauled his kayak for him. They had cached them all in the same place the autumn before, when the ice froze solid. The old man was excited to see his kayak again. He chattered and chuckled while they examined the boat skin for damage. Aneze couldn't understand anything he said now. He was too busy with his kayak.

It was a small boat. Aneze could see that it was very different from her own people's boats. The bottom was rounded, so the boat rested on its side. It was covered in sealskin. And not just on the bottom and the sides. No, this boat had sealskin covering the top part too, except for a little hole. She peered inside the hole. The old man noticed her.

He spoke to her in her own language. "I made it from driftwood. It was difficult collecting enough drift-wood for a kayak. A kayak is a precious thing." Aneze thought it was a beautiful thing. Like the woman's beautiful coat.

"Want to test it out?" The old man asked her. The other hunters were listening, waiting for her response.

"Yes, please," she said. "Will you show me how?"

"First, pick it up."

Aneze hesitated. It was small, but it was not that small. Was the old man joking with her? Everyone was watching. She tried to pick it up. *WHOOSH*! Hey! It wasn't heavy at all! Everyone laughed. She turned this way and that. There were cries of "ai, ai" and "look out" and more laughter as the hunters dodged the swinging kayak.

"Be careful, Ahwak," the old man chuckled. "It's a kayak, not a club."

"Eh, excuse me," she told everyone. "But it's so light!" she exclaimed to the old man. He made her put it down and he peeled back some of the boat skin. There was nothing there, just a few pieces of wood tied together. They were planning to hunt Caribou in this? It didn't seem too sturdy.

"Here, put this on." The old man handed her an odd sort of coat, also made from sealskin. The old man had changed into a pair of long boots that covered his legs up past his thighs.

"My son, Alareak, loans you his kayak-tunic. He only wears it on sea journeys. But while you learn, it will keep you drier." Some of the others decided they would join in the fun too. The children came down to the shore to watch. Aneze heard cries back and forth between the tents as she followed the old man and the kayak into the gray water. She watched the others jump into the small holes at the tops of their boats before the water even reached their ankles. The old man steadied her kayak and she climbed in too. Then he pushed her and the kayak into deeper water. Was it wobbly! She heard comments and laughter from the shore. Even wives had left their work to see the orphan hunter try the kayak for the first time.

She watched the others out in the middle of the river. They whipped around. Those double paddles helped them go really fast. Aneze wanted to try that. She watched while the men splashed and tried to capsize each other. One hunter paddled to shore. His little girl hopped onto the back of the kayak and he took off. She looked like she was riding a big seal. She squealed with joy. Aneze wanted to get out there too.

"Not so fast," the old man warned. "You need to learn how to come back up if you tip over."

He showed her how to lie away from her kayak, on the water. The kayak stuck fast to her lower body. It twisted to one side, but it held her. It was a nice feeling. She felt like a water animal now—unsinkable. She felt like a seal with a big kayak tail.

"That's right. Now you must get back up."

The old man showed her how to slide her shoulders from the water, onto the back of the kayak. The boat just twisted upright again. It was easy. This boat wasn't wobbly; it moved like a fish. It was part of the water. The big water-tail kept her afloat while her top part wiggled around and controlled it.

The old man showed her how to lean forward, wrap her arms under the boat and hug her new water-tail. He tipped the boat over so her tail was in the air and her top part was under the water. The special tunic hood was snug around her face. Not much water got in. He steadily spun her around and around. She was in the air, she was under water, in the air, under water. Breathe in, breathe out, breathe in, breathe out. It was magic! It was like turning into a sea creature! What a boat!

He taught her how to capsize herself so that she hung upside down under the water. He showed her how to use the double paddle to twist herself back up into the air, with her tail under her again. He made her practice, over and over again. Only then did he let her paddle out to where the others played.

She capsized. Looked like she needed to practice.

But then suddenly someone was shouting from the shore. Everyone stopped their splashing to listen.

"Caribou!"

Aneze knew that word by now. Caribou had been spotted. The herd was headed for the crossing point, upriver. They would be there soon. Everyone paddled to shore. It was time to get ready for the hunt.

Caribou

EVERYONE WAS getting ready for Caribou.

The old man tested the edge of his spearhead with his thumb. The woman in the beautiful coat sharpened her skinning knife. Aneze laughed to watch the children at their new game. They collected old pieces of antler and bone, which were scattered all over the ground. Some of the children held these to their heads and ran this way and that. Then little hunters with invisible spears chased the stubby little caribou. Yes, everyone in camp was excited and busy.

But all the activity wasn't just for Caribou. It was because of something else. Aneze felt it too.

Everyone's eyes stayed wide open, and their feet never tired, because the light was long and it kept everything awake. Even the little flowers and grasses grew while Aneze watched. Everything was so happy to see the sun. Caribou was happy too. The cows were on the move from the birthing grounds. Caribou always moved, looking for new grasses to graze.

Aneze was going to eat Caribou again! The grown hunters kayaked across the river to their hiding place. The older boys who could manage their kayaks followed. There was no kayak for Aneze. The old man wouldn't have allowed her to go anyway; she didn't have the skill for it. She stayed with the children and the wives. Everyone waited as the herd approached.

It was beautiful. First, Aneze heard them. They made a low thunder. Their wide hooves beat the ground. Then they appeared. Their coats were scraggly and full of holes. Warble Fly's babies made the holes. From under Caribou's skin, safe and warm, they were burrowing out of their winter nests. In autumn, Caribou would be fat again and have strong new coats. Right now, people weren't hunting for skins. This hunt was just for tasting.

What fun to see Caribou again! In the forest with her family, Aneze had followed them all winter long. Seeing Caribou was like seeing home.

Aneze sat with the others on their side of the river. They remained still and quiet, watching the herd approach the far side. Far across the river, the hunters waited in their kayaks. The first of the herd reached the riverbank. They stopped. They flicked their noses in the air. They trotted back and forth along the riverbank. The herd began piling up from the back. The hunters continued to wait, still and silent. Caribou didn't like to cross rivers. Strong river currents might carry the little ones away. Sometimes wolves or people waited in ambush. Aneze held her breath while the herd hesitated.

Finally the first cow plunged into the water. Her calf stayed by her side. One or two slowly followed… and then more and more. The crossing had begun. When a great many were well into the river, the old man gave the sign from his kayak. The hunters raced to get out among the herd. The fastest paddlers had the advantage. Everyone looked for the biggest and fattest cows. Most were thin from nursing their babies.

The hunters glided among them. They drove their spears into the swimming animals. Some fought hard. Some lay on their sides and kicked out with their hooves. Others gave great lunges to escape. The hunters had to paddle their hardest just to keep up. It was better to look for a quieter animal. Bodies floated on the water now, but the great herd kept coming.

When the front of the herd reached the opposite shore, Aneze and the others stood up. They waved their arms and shouted. They jumped up and down. The startled animals turned back into the water. They bumped into others heading for the shore. Which way to go? There were hunters in the water and there was something alarming on shore. In all this confusion, the hunters were able to kill more.

The herd flowed around both sides of the commotion. They were like a gray furry river of their own. Even as she shouted and hoped for more kills, Aneze loved watching Caribou clatter their long legs out of the water and up onto the bank. She especially loved to watch the babies tripping and climbing. They called for their mothers to come and find them. Finally the last of the animals clambered up the banks. They loped off to the comfort of their trail. Another river crossed.

It was a small group. Aneze had seen herds so large that days and days would pass before all the animals had gone by. Aneze watched this herd continue along its path. Almost like nothing had happened to it. You couldn't really stop Caribou. Caribou went on forever.

Then, what a feast they had!

Every hunter had caribou meat for his family. They all stuffed themselves. The fresh livers went first, and the hearts, kidneys and tongues. Mmmm! The women made a soup from the heads. The fat behind the eyes was especially good. Bones were cracked for their rich marrow. After the ribs were skinned, it was very nice to cut chunks from the flesh and pop them in your mouth, just like that. Aneze had never tasted raw caribou meat before. It was delicious. It was tender and the flavor was mild. It was much nicer than raw seal meat. The old man looked up from his own meal. His mouth was all bloody.

"Now we will all smell nice," he said. "People who eat Caribou smell better than people who eat Seal."

Soon some people dragged themselves off for a nap. Others sat around drinking tea. Wives were busy with their caribou leftovers. Some parts would be cached in a pile of stones to keep out Bear, Wolf and Fox. Some parts would be sliced thin and hung from the tent lines to dry in the sun.

Finally the sun dipped underground for a quick rest. Aneze followed the old man into their tent.

"Your people hunt Caribou much the same way mine do," Aneze said.

"Oh, is that right?"

"Yes, sometimes we also drive them into a trap. We make fences with sticks."

"We do that too." The old man nodded. "Only we make piles of rocks. Caribou run away from them, toward our hunters."

"Do you think it's true?" Aneze settled herself under her sleeping fur. "The story of the first mother, the one who crossed?"

"I don't know that story," he replied.

"My grandmother told it to me. Well, she's not really my grandmother, but we all called her Grandmother. She was so old, you know. She told us that the first mother had to leave her home. There was some kind of trouble. She walked with her two children. They walked until they couldn't walk anymore. They stood in front of a great wide water. They couldn't see the other side."

"Is that so?"

"Yes, and the mother didn't know what to do, because they could not turn back. But then Wolf came and spoke to her. Wolf told them to follow him across the water. The mother said to her children, 'What else can we do?' When they walked across the water, they saw that it was only a few inches deep. They walked and walked until they reached a new land."

"So what happened?"

"Well, when they reached the new land, they killed a lone caribou and ate it. Wolf told them which way to walk from there. The mother said to her children, 'It's time to go now. We must follow Caribou.' But one of the children, his mouth all covered with Caribou's blood, said he didn't want to leave. So the mother and the other child left. Grandmother said this other child became the first of our people. The one who stayed behind is the first of the people of the snow." Aneze shrugged. "I thought maybe the people of the snow meant you."

She wasn't sure she was supposed to tell that story. It was elders who told stories. Young people didn't know enough yet.

"I never heard that story." The old man broke up a lump of fat in the fire oil. It was caribou fat—it did smell better. "It's a good story." He climbed under his sleeping fur. "That would make us the same people, way back," he mused.

Aneze sat up. She didn't want to sleep yet. She had decided something, out there by the river, when she was jumping up and down with the wives and children. Well, she didn't know that she had decided it at the time, but now she realized it was true.

"I'd like to go back," she said. "I'd like to go back to the forest." She felt sad as she said it, but she still meant it. The old man sat back up. He looked her straight in the eye for a while...for a long while. He didn't seem angry. Still, it was nerve-racking. She tried to look straight back. Then she looked at the fire.

"Yes, all right," he said finally.

Suddenly Aneze regretted the idea. "I'll come back to visit," she blurted out. "We could kayak some more, couldn't we?"

"Yes, all right." He smiled a little. "And if you don't come back, I will come fetch you!"

Aneze smiled a little too. She hugged herself. She looked around the tent. It was skin now; there wasn't much snow anymore. What a very long winter it had been.

"Thank you, Magician." It was the first time she had said it out loud—that she knew he was magic. The old man broke out laughing.

"I'm not a magician!"

"Yes, you are." Aneze felt very shy, but she said it anyway. "You can't fool me."

The old man laughed again. "You'll make a good hunter, Ahwak, my young hunting partner."

It was time to tell him the truth. He had been very kind. Aneze wanted him to know.

"I'm not really a hunter," she admitted.

There was a long silence.

People didn't like being tricked. He'd taught her so many things a hunter must know. And here she was, just a girl after all. She was scared to look up. Finally she dared to peek.

He wasn't mad. He wasn't even surprised. Had he known all along? He was just looking at her, as if he had been waiting to meet her eyes.

"Yes, you are a hunter," he told her. Then he smiled. "You can't fool me."

Wolf

BACK IN the woods again.

On the return journey, it had seemed to Aneze that they traveled much faster and farther than they ever had before. It all happened in a whirl. Every time she woke from a rest, they seemed to be in a different place from where they had lain down. Perhaps it was necessary to leave the old man's world while sleeping. Or perhaps her mind was playing tricks because she was traveling through lands where she had once been so lost and alone, before he had found her. Before he rescued her.

Aneze had changed her mind about going back many times. But the old man wouldn't let her. He kept the dogs pointed toward her world. Sometimes she worried that he was punishing her for wanting to leave. Other times she thought he was helping her stick to her decision.

It was a good season to return. All the animals were out. It was the season of birds and eggs. The blackflies and mosquitoes were almost gone, but the days were still warm. It was strange to be among the trees again. It seemed crowded. But she was getting used to it. It was so easy to make a fire. She didn't need to carry a stone lamp anymore, just her flint. Making a lean-to was easy too. She just cut some branches, laid on some spruce boughs, and there! A shelter fit for a hunter.

If only the old man had decided to stay in the forest for a while. If only he had decided to keep her company, just to make sure that she could really take care of herself. The old man had given her the sealskin suit, for keeps. She wore it all the time—the short trousers, parka and boots. The suit made Aneze feel good, special. It also kept the water off her better than anything else. She touched the smooth fur of the hood. She remembered what he had said before he left her on the barren ground to go back to his own icy world.

"This is for you, Orphan Ahwak," and he handed her a small stone. "Sew it into your hood."

Aneze looked at the stone. It fit easily in the palm of her hand. When she looked more closely, she saw that it was a tiny white carved bear.

"That bear in your hand will give you bear powers—

bear strength, bear speed. Bear hunts alone. Now you will too."

Aneze nodded. "Perhaps I'm being foolish to think of staying in the forest?" She waited. Would he relent and tell her to stay with him? Would he say that she was going to be fine by herself? It was ridiculous, but Aneze wanted him to say both things.

"Orphans must be especially strong," he told her. "I think the white bear will help. But I think you must find your own animal." The old man looked around. He sighed. "I think maybe you will meet your animal in your world, not mine."

"Oh. Yes. Well," Aneze said. Then this was good-bye.

"Remember, Ahwak." The old man closed her hand over the white bear. He held on for a moment. "You have lost your ancestors, but you may have descendants yet. Be strong. Become wise. And see that you deserve them." The old man smiled and winked. Then he was gone.

He was right. The white bear did help. She caught fish in her net. She shot birds with her slingshot. She trapped rabbits in her snares. Once she saw Moose in the forest. What a feast that would be. She made a spear for herself and practiced throwing it at tree trunks. She stretched and dried her rabbit skins. She made a pretty bag out of bird skin. She kept her sewing needles in it.

When she got cuts or scrapes, she covered them with spruce sap. She made a pot out of tree-skin. When she wanted boiled meat, she heated stones in the fire and dropped them in the pot of water. When she wanted roasted meat, she buried it in the fire. She kept her spear and her knife sharp. She tried to remember what her mother knew, and she tried to remember what her father knew. She was very busy. She wasn't even bothered by the hollow inside, not much anyway. She wasn't even scared, not very.

Except once.

Aneze was camped by the shores of a big lake. It was getting dark, so she set up a fire pit. Then she saw a red glow, far away, along the shore. A campfire. And then another flickered in the black sky, and another. People! So many fires meant many people! Aneze stopped her work. If she lit her fire, they would see it for sure. They could be enemies. Even if they were not enemies, they might not like her. They would know she was bad luck—an orphan. They might pretend to be kind and try to kill her in her sleep. She knew how these things worked. It was best to stay hidden. But she needed her fire. What to do? Hmm, hm, hm.

It was too dark to travel away from the lake. She touched the hem of her hood, where the stone bear lived.

Bear didn't hide from anyone. But Rabbit hid all the time. She reached for a rabbit fur. Rabbit had no ideas for her. She should have known—that was just like Rabbit. But she had forgotten Fox! She shook some fox teeth out of her pocket. She jostled them in her hand.

"Uhmmm, uhmm, uhmm." Aneze sang a little song to encourage them. "Uhmm, uhmm, ah-uhmm." The fox teeth jumped out of her hand and scattered all over the ground. Of course! Fox was so clever. Many fires. Aneze had to build many fires, all around her campsite. More fires than those others had burning. She would make herself look like many people, more than they were. That would frighten those others and keep them away. Aneze gathered up Fox's teeth and put them back in her pocket. It was time to gather more wood.

THE DAYS WERE still hot, but night came quickly now. The spring and summer season always slipped by in a blink. Aneze wanted to try hunting big animals, like a true hunter. In all her travels, she had not seen Caribou. Soon the herd would be coming back to the forest. She had no idea how to meet it. She needed a caribou suit for the winter. If she was going to be a hunter, she had to hunt Caribou.

"One day, you will hunt without me," Aneze remembered Father telling Brother. "When you are ready, you must look for your dream-vision. You will recognize it, because your animal will make himself known to you in this dream. A hunter who knows his animal can understand himself—his own strengths, the way he should hunt. A hunter who has no dream-vision is never really grown."

That must be the problem. Aneze didn't know her own animal. How could she know Caribou if she didn't even know her own animal? The old man had told her much the same thing. With the help of her animal, she could learn to be strong and wise. Her animal might even help her find and hunt Caribou.

Aneze decided it was time to seek her dream-vision. Normally a young hunter went off on his own for the first time and didn't come back until he'd dreamed his dream-vision. But Aneze was already alone. She needed to do something different. She stopped fishing and trapping. She started wandering. She took no particular path—she just followed her nose until it was too dark to travel. Who knew where the dream-vision waited? She ate a little dried meat. She slept. She didn't do much besides that. She didn't want to be too busy fixing a net or stalking a bird to notice her vision.

Soon Aneze wandered less and less. She enjoyed just sitting. Sometimes she sat on a log. She liked to sit by a river or a lake. Once she spent the whole day watching Frog. That was an odd thing to do. But Frog wasn't bothered. He carried on his business as if he was all by himself. In fact, Aneze realized, birds acted this way too. They hopped right by her, looking for grubs to eat. They didn't flap and fly away. She stood up and walked into the river. She waited for the fish to come. They swam right through her legs, brushing up against them like they were fallen branches.

Strange…It was as if she wasn't there. She climbed back out again. Had she turned into a ghost? Aneze thumped her arms and her chest. No, it was all right, she was really there.

Then she heard a noise in the bush. Something was waiting for her in the trees. She could feel it. Was it an evil sprit? Was it a devil? Maybe it was her animal. Maybe she was dreaming and didn't even know it. Aneze walked toward it. She didn't even worry about being quiet.

She walked into a small clearing. The sun shone all the way down to the ground here. The rocks and needles felt warm under her feet. Wasn't this where the thing had been waiting? She felt very faint. She was too dizzy. Aneze lay down, but she kept her eyes wide open.

Blackness came in around the edges anyway. The peep-
hole through which she could see became smaller and
smaller. A sound grew louder in her ears—*hiss-
WHOOSH*. It sounded like her own breathing, only it
was bigger and inside her head.

Then she felt as if she was speeding. She was going
faster than the old man's dogsled—faster even than
Eagle could fly. But wait, the trees were whizzing by in
a blur, yet she felt no wind. Actually, it didn't seem like
she was moving at all; it seemed like the forest was
rushing past her. And just as she thought "This is not
possible. Forests don't run," she was somewhere else.

Now she was somewhere dark, damp and warm.
It looked like the ribs of an animal. Was she speeding
through the ribs of some huge animal? Yes, she could
see it breathing—expanding and contracting, in, out,
in, out. *Hiss-WHOOSH*. So this was where that sound
had been coming from! But she was there only an
instant, and then it all slipped away. She sped right
through to the light. Or the light came toward her.
It seemed as if everything else was moving, while she
remained perfectly still. And then suddenly she was
on the hill.

Or rather, she wasn't. She could see it, but she
wasn't really there. It was bright. It was bright, bright,
bright from the sun and the snow. But she didn't

feel the cold. It was clean here. There were no tracks, no rocks, no mud. The snow glittered and twinkled like stars. She was on the top of a crest. It fell away sharply on both sides.

She was looking along the tip-top of a mountain range. She had never seen anything like it. She had never been so high. She couldn't see the bottom. The tips of the mountains spread out before her. They looked like the backbone of some gigantic creature. This was an empty world, but Aneze wasn't scared. It wasn't a lonely place—it was complete. It didn't need anyone to see it. It was beautiful. A voice spoke inside her head. It was her own voice.

"This must be the spine of the world."

At that moment, she saw something coming toward her along the top of the crest. It ran fast, but easily, in great loping strides. It was Wolf. His fur was white. Wolf saw her. He was running toward her. He was looking right at her. She looked back into his eyes.

They were not kind eyes. But they did not seem to be angry either. Wolf's thick coat rippled over his shoulders as he ran. It captured the light of the sun and held it. He was coming. She wanted to turn and run. But she couldn't move, she wasn't really there. His eyes held hers as if he recognized her. He seemed to say, "You, wait there, I'm coming." He pinned her in place.

Aneze wished hard that his eyes might soften toward her, even just a little. But they didn't. And then he was upon her.

Suddenly, Aneze was back in the clearing. She bolted upright. Through the trees she saw him. His coat was gray now, and his mate was with him. They both looked at her—those eyes. Then they turned away. Aneze struggled to her feet and walked over to where they had been. They had been eating something. They'd caught Caribou! They'd eaten out the tongue and the liver, but there was so much left over!

Aneze took out her knife and sliced off a tender morsel by the rib. She ate it right then, just like the old man. Just like Wolf. She ate only a little bit; her belly needed to get used to food again. Aneze chewed and chewed. She thought about her dream-vision. Grandmother had told stories about hunters and their animals. She told a story about a hunter who healed sick people whenever he asked for Caribou's help. Another story was about a hunter who could ask Eagle to tell him where there was food whenever his people were starving. Father never told stories about his animal.

"A hunter doesn't talk about his animal. The power will go away. If he is in serious trouble—about to drown, maybe, or get killed by a bear—a hunter will remember his first meeting with his animal. The memory will give him extra strength so that he may survive."

Aneze sure wasn't going to forget her vision. Wolf was special—a strong and good animal. Wolf was smart; he could even tell what others were thinking. Aneze would like to be able to do that. Perhaps one day Wolf would give her special powers too.

But for now, Aneze would take care of the gift that Wolf had given her. She set to work cutting away the skin. It would make a blanket, or perhaps a winter shirt. Later she would drag a haunch back to where she had left her things, right by Frog, beside the river. She would build a fire. She would be drying meat for many days. Her animal had come.

People

AFTER THAT, Aneze consulted Wolf whenever she could.

When she heard wolves call, she always answered. She didn't sound quite the same as Wolf, she knew that. She sounded quite a bit like a person. But the wolves never minded that. They let her join in, just the same. Were they finding each other in the forest? Were they warning each other away from their hunting grounds? Or were they calling just for the joy of hearing their own howlish song?

One time, Aneze was howling to some friends in the distance when she heard a new voice. It sounded almost like Wolf, but not quite. It sounded just like her. Another person!

Aneze's heart jumped around in her chest. She tried to slow her breath. There were people nearby! Were they good people or not? Wolf hunted in a pack.

Wolves cared for each other. They had families. They were able to kill Caribou only because they worked together. They shared meat with each other. Aneze gathered her bundle and tied it to her back. She followed the people-howl. She picked her way carefully. She didn't want to make noise. Surely this was a good person, a person who talked to wolves. Right?

She smelled fire. It was over there. Aneze crept closer. Two hunters had a camp. The older one was drinking tea by the fire. The younger one was a little way off, howling to Wolf. Aneze crept closer still. They seemed to be kind people. They looked comfortable together—content. They looked like her people, not like enemies. But she couldn't be sure.

"Ketchwatin, come drink some tea and leave those wolves in peace. They don't need you barking and yipping like a fool pup." The older hunter waved a steaming bowl at the boy.

Aneze shivered a little inside her sealskin parka. It was getting chilly, now that the sun was down. The man spoke the language of her people. Not exactly the same, but she understood him. She would give them a try.

Aneze stood up. She crackled a few warning branches and stepped into the firelight, Both hunters jumped up like rabbits. The man held a knife. The boy reached for a spear on the ground.

"No war," Aneze said, trying out her people-voice for the first time in a while. It sounded funny to her ears. She cleared her throat and tried again.

"No war." She stood stock-still. Neither hunter moved, their eyes wide. They were scared—she could smell it. Didn't they hear her greeting? Aneze didn't like that spear. It could hit her at this distance. She moved *veerrrry* slowly. She pulled off her hood and bowed her head to show that she was friendly.

"No war?" She tried again. The older hunter squinted at her and shifted his weight. The boy threw his spear, just as the hunter cried, "Wait—it's just a girl!"

The spear wobbled, but it was too late. It landed shy of catching her smack in the chest, but it did nick her on the leg as it came down. Luckily, her sealskin trousers took most of the damage.

"*Aieee!*" she cried. "Why do you want to kill me? I said 'no war' already—three times!"

The hunter laughed and laughed. The boy looked between the two of them. Aneze was on the ground, examining her leg. The hunter was bent over, holding his sides and wheezing with laughter.

"Ai! Ketch and I thought for sure you were a ghost—ha, ha, ha!" He caught his breath and wiped his eyes. "You should see yourself, popping out of the bush like that, all in white—what is that you're wearing?

You gave us a good fright—hee, hee."

Aneze looked down at herself. It was true. She must look odd in the old man's sealskins. There were no other sealskins in the forest. Seal didn't live in this world. Her clothes weren't really white; they were gray. But in the dark, all by herself, with her hood on, she must have looked scary. She started to laugh too.

"Well, it's not funny!" the boy said, huffing and puffing. "It's not at all funny. What if I'd killed you?" He walked over to Aneze. He sneaked a peek at the gash in her leg before he grabbed his spear and walked away.

"Father, stop laughing. Please see if I hurt her." He turned back to Aneze. "What are you doing by yourself? Where is your mother? Or your husband?"

Aneze stood up. Although it hurt a great deal, she acted like she didn't feel a thing. "I hope there was no poison on that spear, or you have killed me," she said as calmly as she could. It had been a long time since anyone had talked to her as if she was a girl.

"Hee, hee, hee," the hunter laughed as he took his seat again. "Come here, ghost. Sit down, drink some spruce-needle tea. That will fix you up."

Aneze stared long and hard at the boy. He refused to look back. He started to sharpen the spearhead.

"I'll just get some sap for my leg," she said.

"Oh, let Ketchwatin get it for you. You rest the

leg for a bit. It's going to be fine. There's no poison on that spear."

But Aneze said, "Hey, it barely hurts. I can get it myself." She collected her own spruce sap with her own knife. She tried not to limp.

When she was by the fire, she applied it to her leg. Both hunters carefully looked away.

"You are used to looking after yourself, huh?" The older hunter offered her some tea. "What's your name, skinny?"

Aneze sipped the tea. Bitter. Good. It chased away sickness and infection from the inside. "My name is Ahwak," she told them. "I'm an orphan." She turned to the boy. "That answers your nosy question about my mother."

"Now, now, don't fight," the hunter said. "Let's everybody be friends. We're not used to seeing girls wandering around the woods. Not real live ones, anyway, right, Ketch?" Ketchwatin looked up at his father with a small smile. "We must have looked pretty silly, huh, Pa? Knees shaking, mouths open, bugs flying in?" Then he made a face like he was so scared—eyes crossed, mouth stretched wide. This time everybody laughed.

Much later, Aneze drifted off to sleep in her own lean-to, across the fire from the hunters. From somewhere far away, she thought she heard Wolf howl.

Root

HER FOOT was good and stuck.

Aneze had tried wiggling it. But she had only wedged it deeper between the tree root and the ground. Now it hurt. She had scraped her ankle with all her twisting. She watched the blood ooze from the scrape. By now Ketch would surely realize that she wasn't right behind him. He was carrying the ax. The ax would hack this root off her, once and for all.

How ridiculous. Getting stuck like this, with nothing to cut herself free. She tried to shake the root loose with both hands, but it was old and tough. It wound around the great rock underground. When it couldn't find a way below ground, it had simply come above. It grew like that, along the ground. Then it found a soft spot and tucked itself into the earth again. It was a perfect snare for a careless foot.

She had been racing after Ketch. He always wanted to be in the bush, away from camp. He'd grabbed the ax and mumbled something about getting wood. That was just an excuse. Getting wood was women's work. Aneze knew he was going off to have fun. Fishing, climbing, exploring. Aneze wanted some fun too!

"I'll help!" She jumped up and ran after Ketch before anyone could find her something else to do. She hadn't even stopped to get her knife.

When would Ketch come back? What bad luck that she had stepped on that rotted log. That it had given way like that. That her foot had twisted just so and gotten wedged under the root. Bad luck. The scrape was really stinging too. Ketch would be along any time now. There was nothing to do but wait.

That's when she noticed Wolverine—two shiny eyes over a black snout—peeking from under the bush. He was hiding, but she saw him now. He might have been watching her for some time. He might already know she was stuck. If he knew, she was in big trouble. Wolverine wasn't large, but he was strong. He could easily tear her apart, stuck like this. Maybe he wasn't too hungry. Maybe he'd rather wait to find meat that was already dead. That would be less trouble for him.

Hunters admired Wolverine. Many dreamed him as their animal. They tried to copy his strength, his determination. Wolverine was clever. Everybody knew that. He was the trickster. Aneze had been told lots of stories about Wolverine and his tricks. He was fierce, he was brave and he could disappear whenever he liked.

She had to appear strong. She needed Wolverine's respect if she were to have any chance of keeping him away. She looked him straight in the eyes. She could see his eyes and his nose through the branches. He looked like a bear cub.

Oh, if only he were!

He crept out from the bushes. Now she could see the pale stripes that ran along his body and all the way down his long bushy tail.

Aneze tried to look big. She sat up tall. She puffed up her tunic. Wolverine advanced a few steps, sizing her up. He didn't look worried.

Keeping her eyes on him, Aneze tried to get her back against the tree trunk. She couldn't turn completely because of her foot. But she was better covered than before. Now Wolverine would have a hard time attacking from behind.

That didn't seem to bother him. He took a few steps closer, still curious, still deciding.

Aneze fumbled around on the ground for sticks and rocks—anything of a good size. She brought them in, close to her sides. Stay tall. Don't look away. Should she be the first to strike? Or would that goad him to attack?

But if she waited for him to strike, surely she wouldn't even get in one good blow. His claws and teeth would be in her. Shouldn't she try to bluff him away before he tasted her blood? She felt for her weapons. There was the big stick. Keep that in hand, that'll drive him off. Stones were good for throwing. She felt the heavy one, just at her side. She'd rather keep that one too.

Wolverine was closing in. Aneze threw a fistful of pebbles and leaves. The pebbles rained around Wolverine and the leaves whirled in a blur. Wolverine braced himself. It looked like they were going to fight.

Aneze took several breaths. She felt cold suddenly and wide awake. Her foot had stopped hurting.

"Come on," she yelled at Wolverine. "You want some of my stick? My stone?" She brandished each one so he could see. "I'll use your pelt to trim my hood!" she bellowed.

Wolverine's nose lifted in the air. In a flash, he jumped.

Aneze drove him back with her stick. With a snarl, he got it between his teeth and shook it hard. He whipped his head from side to side. Oh no! Had he popped her arm out of her shoulder? She reached out with her other hand and smashed the big stone against his skull as hard as she could. That shook him off her for a moment. Aneze flexed her shoulder. What a relief. It still worked, but she shifted the stick to her other hand. She hoped this arm would be stronger. She readied herself for the next attack.

WHOOMP!

It came from the side, slicing through the air, razor sharp. Aneze couldn't believe it—handle over edge, handle over edge. It was a gift from above. Ketch's ax! It landed at her feet. Aneze grabbed at it and hacked through the root in a few strokes. She was free! She scrambled to her feet and faced Wolverine. But Wolverine wasn't up to this new fight. He turned and loped away. She was a meal not worth the trouble.

Ketch appeared. He was pale and sweating.

"I didn't know what to do," he gasped. "I wanted to kill him! I'm sure I could have!" He stared after Wolverine. "But what if I had missed him, Ahwak?" He turned to Aneze, his eyes big. "So I gave you the ax instead."

Aneze couldn't speak. She felt shaky. She sat down. "Aieeee…eee!"

Oh no, was she crying? It was the look on Ketch's face that did it. He looked so scared, so worried. Worried for her…for her.

"Ooooo…hooo!" This wasn't just water from the eyes. She was crying so hard, tears were coming out of her nose.

"I'm sorry, Ahwak." Ketch reached down to pat her on the shoulder. She felt him tapping, light and fast. "I let him get away."

"Nooo…ooo," she choked out. She shook her head. It wasn't that. She didn't care about that.

Oh, the sounds she was making! She never cried like this. Not since she had found Mother crumpled off the path. Ketch was sorry? She was the sorry one! Bad luck she was, nothing but trouble.

Stupid root! Stupid foot!

"It's all right. It's all right now." Ketch waited. "Feeling better now?"

Aneze took great shuddering gulps. "Ooooo… hooo!" Ketch didn't know. He didn't understand. He always shared his adventures. He always had help. He had no idea what he had done for her.

She should stop crying now. Ketch was getting scared. She tried, but she just ended up making funny snorting noises.

"I'm going to get Ma," she heard him say.

"No, Ketch!" she cried out. He turned around.

Aneze made a great effort to calm down. "Please don't leave me. Please?"

He paused. Then he nodded. He came back and sat down beside her. She could feel the warmth of his arm against her arm, his leg against her leg. That helped. He didn't scold her about forgetting her knife. He didn't say anything about her bad luck. She snorted and snuffled a little bit more.

Ketch said, "It's fine now, Ahwak. It always comes out all right. See?"

She was breathing easier now. No more funny sounds.

Ketch leaned over, trying to peer into her face. "I heard you shouting, before. 'I'll use your pelt to trim my hood!'" he mimicked her. "Nice war talk, Ahwak. Very tough."

Ketch thought he was so funny. Aneze jabbed her elbow into his ribs.

"Oof! Aah!" He faked and fell over. "You should have tried that on Wolverine!" he moaned from the ground.

Aneze couldn't help but smile. What a silly. She wiped her face on her sleeve. It always comes out all right, he'd said. She let herself believe him for a moment.

Camp

"THERE, YOU'VE got him! Uh-oh, nooo, not like that! Oh, ai, you're letting him get away!"

Ketch laughed as Aneze scrambled across the creek after Wiggly Frog. Mud splattered. Then *splash*! Aneze landed face-first in the creek.

"Got him!" she cried. "He's fast! If I can ever get him tied, he's going to beat your frog for sure!"

Ketch looked at his own frog. It sat in his hand, quite still. He gave it a poke. Still Frog refused to budge. Aneze had a good point.

"Bring him over here. I'll show you again." Ketch tucked his frog in his pocket. "Do you have the sewing-thread?" Ketch tied the special knot again. Only this time he slipped it around Aneze's frog. He tied it snug, but not too tight. It went just behind the short front legs. He put Wiggly Frog on the ground.

"Aaiiee!" Aneze cried. Wiggly Frog was making his escape. This time it was easy for Aneze to catch the end of the sewing-thread.

"I might look for another frog," Ketch said.

"Oh no, let's do one race first, Ketch," Aneze said. "We're all ready to go."

"It won't be any fun," Ketch argued. "My frog isn't going anywhere. Of course you will win."

"Well, let's just try one time," Aneze pleaded. "It took us so long to find these two. Just once? One race only, all right? Please?"

Ketch narrowed his eyes. A shadow crossed his face. He pulled Still Frog out of his pocket. "All right, one race," he sighed. "But it doesn't count. This one won't count. It's just a practice race."

"Eeee!" Aneze cheered. "Let's go!"

"Wait. First we have to make a racecourse," Ketch told her. "Something long and narrow, so they won't jump in all directions." He scouted around. "A hollow log. Or a piece of tree-skin, if it's the right size."

They scouted for a while. The frogs were tucked safely in their pockets. They came to the place where rock grew out of the ground.

"Maybe we could dig a racecourse back by the creek bed," Aneze suggested.

Ketch looked at her sideways. He raised one eyebrow.

"Maybe *you* could dig a racecourse. You're covered in mud already—oh wait!" he cried. "Never mind. Look, Ahwak, it's perfect!"

In between two great rocks under their feet, a long shallow trench had formed. It was just wide enough for two mud frogs to race side by side.

"This is good! This is perfect for racing." Ketch's face shone like a star. He must have forgotten about his frog's chances of winning.

They both crouched down. They set the frogs at one end of the trench. Aneze had to hold on tight to Wiggly Frog. Still Frog stayed still.

"One, two, three, go!"

Aneze and Ketch let go of their strings. Wiggly Frog leaped and leaped down the trench. Still Frog sat.

"Go! Go!"

"Come on, come on!"

Both of them urged their frogs on. Ketch poked at Still Frog with a stick. "You see, I told you!" He was turning red.

Then Wiggly Frog made a leap to escape up the low wall of the trench. He didn't make it. He landed on his back. When he flipped over, he turned himself around. Wiggly Frog headed back to the starting point. *Leap, leap, leap*.

"No! No!" Aneze cried. "Go the other way!"

"Come on, come on!" Ketch started up with the stick again, prodding Still Frog.

"No, stop! Go back!" Aneze was half laughing, half crying. Wiggly Frog was very frustrating.

"What happens if he jumps out the wrong end, Ketch?"

"Well, then my frog wins, doesn't he?" Ketch laughed.

Then something funny happened. Wiggly Frog was almost hopping past the starting point. He was on his way to a spectacular defeat. Suddenly, Still Frog jumped up onto Wiggly Frog's back. Wiggly Frog tried to wiggle away, but Still Frog kept pushing himself back on with his strong legs. It was a mess of webby feet and long back legs pushing and slipping all over the place. Wiggly's head got stomped by Still's front foot. Aneze laughed to see Wiggly's eyes bulge out in surprise.

"It's not a race, it's a wrestling match!" Ketch cried. "Get him! Pin him to the ground!" Both frogs rolled backward, past the starting point, together. It was a tie for second place.

"Ha! Ha!" Ketch punched the air. Still Frog had done pretty well, considering.

"Again, again!" Aneze shouted. They gathered up their frogs. Only somehow, in the scuffle, Still Frog's sewing-thread had snapped.

"How about you try to sneak more thread from Mother?" Ketch suggested. "I'll go look for a real racing frog this time."

"Good idea," Aneze said. "Meet you back at the creek."

ANEZE WAS COMING around the tent, toward the fire pit, when something made her stop. Aunt and Uncle were talking. Somehow she sensed they were talking about her. She crept a little nearer. She kept close to the shadow of the tent.

"Well, you need help with looking after Cub and doing the chores," Uncle was saying.

"Oh, I can handle my work," Aunt said. "But it's true that she needs to learn. Her stitches aren't so good. She's not practicing enough."

"I will tell Ketch to stop playing with her," Uncle said. "He needs to know that girls have a lot of work to do."

"It's just that she's not normal, Husband. How did she manage to survive all that time alone in the bush? And those odd clothes she was wearing. From 'Seal,' she says. What kind of animal is that? I don't know about you, but for me the whole thing is too strange. It could be bad magic."

Aneze knew Aunt would never talk so much without working at the same time. Whatever Aunt was doing, her voice got very low. Aneze couldn't hear what she said next.

"Ahwak is a good girl," Uncle said. Aneze heard that part clearly. "She's smart and she wants to please. She especially wants to please you, Wife."

"I know, I know it. Don't you think I know it?" Aneze could hear her clearly now. Aunt must have stopped her work for a moment. Was she stoking the fire? Cleaning a skin? It was true. Aneze didn't help her enough. Whenever she could, she preferred to be with Ketch. Sometimes Uncle even let her go hunting with them.

"If Ahwak was just some orphan, do you think I could open my heart to her? Let her live with my family? But it worries me. She is an orphan, after all. Her whole family—dead! It's terrible luck. I don't want her passing that luck on to us. And how is it that she's even still alive, a girl on her own? More bad magic, maybe? I think it's eerie."

"It is unusual that she is still here. But it's not impossible," Uncle replied. "Ahwak is strong. She doesn't look it because she hasn't filled out yet. But that girl is strong."

"And she's kind to Cub," Aunt relented. "And Ketch is fond of her. But look, they've been playing in the bush all afternoon now. Who knows what she's been up to?"

"You need more help, that's all." Uncle slapped his thighs. "Ahwak must stop this playing nonsense and grow up, that's all."

"That way I could keep a closer eye on her too." Aunt's voice was so low, Aneze almost didn't catch it. "I don't think she means any harm. I just hope she doesn't bring us any."

Aneze didn't want to beg for more sewing-thread after all.

She turned back toward the creek. She'd been having such fun, she'd forgotten that she had no people of her own. Aunt was right. She was an orphan—an extra—and bad luck besides. Orphans had to work harder, to prove their worth. Orphans didn't have parents who loved them. Aneze took a deep breath. The hollow had suddenly given her a cramp. Funny, she had almost forgotten the hollow was there. She was going to tell Ketch she didn't feel like racing anymore. She was going to let Wiggly Frog go.

Enemies

"AUNT, THE water is ready!" Aneze called into the tent.

"Put the meat into it, will you, Ahwak?" came the reply. "I've almost got this tear sewn up. What is Cub up to? Is he giving you trouble?"

Aneze looked around for Ketch's baby brother, Cub. His chubby legs had carried him over to the old log. It was his favorite spot. There were lots of bugs. At the moment, he was smashing them with a stick.

"He's fine, Auntie. No sign of the men though."

Aunt poked her head out of the tent. The rest of her followed. She was a big strong woman. Not as tall as Mother had been, but bulkier. Aunt never felt the cold.

"If they don't come back soon, we'll eat a little something from the pot." She winked at Aneze. Aneze smiled. Hunters got the first share. Wives ate what was left, if any. But one might snack while preparing the food—

that didn't count. Aneze slid the calf head into the pot. It would make a good soup. She sat back on her heels. Cub was chasing a beetle. She tapped a stick on a rock. She whistled a bit. Aunt was back inside the tent. Ho hum. There was always something to do around camp, but it sure wasn't as much fun as hunting.

"Hunting is too dangerous for you, Ahwak," Aunt said whenever Ahwak asked if she could go hunting with the men.

"Anyway, your aunt needs help with the chores," Uncle said.

Well, Aneze was trying, she really was. She helped Aunt dress the skins the men brought back. She fetched the water and collected the firewood. She carried bundles. She boiled the water. She helped with the mending. But she should be allowed to hunt too, every so often.

The next time Uncle and Ketch set off, she told them, "I'm coming hunting too."

"Excuse me?" Aunt looked shocked. "Ahwak, no one has invited you. Uncle says you are to stay at camp. You've got work to do here. The men don't need you."

Aneze looked over to Uncle. He didn't say anything, but he looked very stern. Ketch was looking every which way. He found a rock to kick. They weren't going to speak up for her? They had first met her in the forest!

They knew she could handle herself. They all knew it.
Everyone was acting crazy.

Aneze went into the tent and found the sealskin
clothes the old man had given her. The old man had
said she was a hunter. She put them on. She collected
her hunting kit. She pulled her hood up over her hair.
She went back outside and just stood there.

Aunt and Uncle exchanged a glance. Then Uncle
shrugged. He walked off. Ketch followed. Aneze
followed too. Nobody said anything else.

Nobody said anything to her all that day.

Uncle asked Ketch, not Aneze, to find him sticks
for the traps. When they came across lynx scat, Uncle
told Ketch to see what the animal had eaten and find
out if he was hungry like they were. He didn't look at
Aneze the whole time.

Who cared about that? Not her. She helped Ketch
build the fire that night. She collected water for tea.
She was hungry, just like them. She, too, hoped the
animals would enter the traps. She cut her own branches
and built her own lean-to. Uncle should understand.
Instead he was mad at her. Why, she'd lived in a world
he'd never even seen!

For another day they laid traps in silence. Uncle's
trapline was long. It ran all the way along one side
of Lake-where-canoe-sank. Then it looped back up past

Old-woman-rapids. It ended along Ridge-where-caribou-like-the-grasses-there. So far they'd had no luck finding anything to hunt along the way. Aneze's stomach rumbled. Maybe they should forget the hunting and try for fish. Uncle was in a foul mood. That night he cursed at Ketch because he and Aneze were too slow building the fire. He didn't say anything to Aneze.

Later, Aneze lay on spruce boughs and listened to the night. She couldn't sleep. She had been all by herself for so long, before. So how come she felt the most lonely right now? She heard a rustle. Ketch was creeping over to her side of the fire.

"Hey, Ahwak," he whispered. "I'm sorry about Father, you know?" Aneze didn't say anything.

"You're a very different kind of person." He tried again. "It's hard for him—for Ma too. They don't know what to do about you." He paused. "I think they are worried about you."

Aneze didn't want Ketch to hear her voice tremble. It was good that it was dark. He wouldn't be able to see her face. She took a breath. "I know I'm different. It doesn't make it easy for me either."

Ketch didn't say anything. But he was still there. He didn't move away.

"Hmm," she finally heard in the darkness. "But you're good, Ahwak. I guess you know that."

She felt water leak from her eyes. She didn't know what to say. Ketch thought she was good. She heard him rustle back to his side of the fire. Aneze went back to looking at the night. She wiped her cheeks dry. She wasn't tired. She would sneak back and see if Uncle's traps had caught anything. If she brought back food in the morning, Uncle would be very happy. Aneze was sure she could reset the traps if she had to, even in the dark.

She waited until she heard Ketchwatin's snores. Then she got up and headed back the way they had come. She found the first trap just fine. It was empty. She headed for the next one. It took a while. The sky lightened while she walked. This trap was also empty. What bad luck! She would check another one. It took even longer to find the next trap. Where had it got to? She'd had no idea it was so close to morning when she had set off. They would be getting up soon. Would Uncle come looking for her? Would he expect her to catch up with them? She didn't want to make any more trouble. She'd better go back.

Everything looked different now that the light was up. Aneze couldn't be sure how far she was from the last trap that she had checked. Had she got herself turned around without noticing? Was she facing the right direction? This was not good. Uncle would be angry. Ketch would probably have a good laugh at her.

If she could just find the second trap, she'd know her way back. But she had better hurry. The sun was coming up. Once she was at the top of the next rise, she was sure she'd recognize her way.

Hm, maybe hurrying was a bad idea. Perhaps she'd passed the second trap already. Should she double back? Now she was really lost.

At least the rising sun told her which way Lake-where-canoe-sank was. Maybe from its shores she could get her bearings. She would just dash over there and have a quick look up and down. She didn't want to lose the others. She didn't want to get left behind. Quickly now!

Snap! *Crackle*! She was almost there—any moment she'd see the water.

Aneze burst through the bush onto the rocks of the shore—Ahhh! Too late!

She saw the enemy canoes too late.

The enemies were all looking at her, weapons ready. Of course they were; she had been thundering through the bush like a beast on fire! She'd lost her head. Aneze dashed back into the wood. The shouts and cries were close behind.

She would dodge them, she would hide—

Zing!

An arrow hissed by her ear. Oh! Oh! Oh! She would

never see Aunt and Uncle again. She ran harder. Some branches whipped across her face. She blinked pine needles out of her eyes. She kept running. Oh! She would never see Cub again—

Zing!

Another arrow whizzed by, this time from another direction. They were cutting her off. She veered, just like Caribou when the wolves were on him. It was hopeless. She ran anyway. She would never see Ketch—

Thunk!

A war ax sank deep into the tree trunk ahead. Still she ran until—

Oof! *Smack*! *Clunk*! Something caught her hard on the ear.

Down she went.

Everything went black. Aneze tried to catch some air. She could hear shouts in the enemy language. She knew what they were saying. Their hunt was successful. She heard laughter.

She felt herself being hauled to her feet. Several hands grabbed at her. Her captors kicked her. She tried to roll into a ball but was jerked up again. Someone grabbed her hair and yanked her head. Someone's face was right up in hers. He was laughing and saying something. He sounded familiar. He smelled familiar. He came into focus.

He had only one eye.

Aneze went cold. She almost blacked out again. She sucked in a breath. Air—she needed more air. He had only one eye. She must stay awake. She must keep the black away. His other eye was all messed up, just an ugly mash of scar skin. A slash mark ran from his forehead, across the cheek, to his ear.

Aneze remembered the cut. She'd tried to get the ear off too. But he had been too fast. He'd twisted her hand until she heard it snap. Then he'd swung her by her feet, knocked her out and thrown her in the creek. The water closed over her now, cool and black. He was shouting something at her, but she didn't care. Her knees gave out. She was back in his grasp, right where it all started. Maybe it had all been a dream. The hunting, the old man, her friend Ketch—maybe they were all just part of a long long dream, under water, here in the cool black.

She was pulled up again—by her hair. The pain woke her up. She must try. She had tried so hard up until now. It was too late to give up now.

Aneze took her chance. She pulled out her knife and slashed it across the arm that held her hair. At the same time she jumped back. She could see she was surrounded. One-Eye rubbed his arm and glared. The other hunters didn't move.

"You can't keep your prisoner!" one of them laughed.

"Is she too much for you, Komoo? Let me have her then—haw haw haw!" Everyone else laughed too.

One-Eye smirked and then lunged, but she jumped aside and sliced at his arm as he reached for her. She aimed for the same spot as before. He cursed at her and examined his arm.

"Ai, you are going to wish you hadn't done that!" He grabbed for her again. But Aneze had already turned and hoisted herself up the nearest tree. It didn't seem like the others were going to stop her.

"Hey, Komoo, you think you can shake her out of that tree? Want me to light a fire, smoke her out for you? Haw haw haw!" Everyone thought this was funny.

"Yeah, if she passes out from the smoke, maybe you'll be able to catch her!"

"Touch me again," Aneze screeched from her tree branch, "and I'll take out your other eye! I will!"

More laughter from below, except from One-Eye. For the first time he looked at her. He really saw her. There it was—she could see it. He finally recognized who she was.

"You know I can do it!" she threatened.

Like a flash, he was up the tree. Murder was on his face.

His companions below egged him on.

"That's the way!"

"Snap her like a twig!"

"Teach her respect!"

Aneze had to get out of there. The only way to go was up. As she climbed, she looked for something—anything—to throw down on him. She had to get him out of the tree. At this height, maybe the fall would kill him.

She climbed. She was smaller than he was. She could crawl out farther onto the branches. What to do? What to do? She tried to ignore the shouts from below. One-Eye tried to scare her with threats as he climbed after her. She wouldn't listen. She had to think.

Then she saw the nest.

Eagle's Child was waiting for Mother and Father to bring food back. He squawked as she crawled up to him... *steady, steady*. He was fully grown, almost ready to fly.

"Hello, Eagle's Child," Aneze chirped. She climbed into the nest. She crunched over bones and fins and snake parts—leftovers from old meals. She saw the claws and beak of the young bird's brother. He had been another meal for Eagle's Child.

"Oh, you're the tough one, aren't you?" Aneze murmured to Eagle's Child. He looked at her with one bright eye. "That's good," she crooned. "Tougher is better."

She peered over the side. She had to get a clear shot. She just needed a shot at his face. That would be enough. She had a good chance.

"Where's she gone? Can you see her up there?" Aneze heard from far below. One-Eye looked up. That was all she needed.

"Time to learn to fly, child," Anezc whispered. She swooped in at his talons and grabbed them tight. His massive wings flapped, but she ducked around them and pinned him close. Then she heaved Eagle's Child out of the nest. It wasn't a great shot; she almost missed One-Eye completely.

But Eagle's Child saw his chance. In his fall, he reached out for One-Eye; he flapped and hung on for dear life. One-Eye tried to protect himself with his injured arm. He grasped the tree with his good arm. He howled and cursed. He tried to shake off Eagle's Child, but the great bird's talons were sunk deep into him. Eagle's Child was terrified—and mad. He pecked at One-Eye's head. One-Eye howled some more.

"Uh-oh, Komoo, you better get down here," Aneze heard from below. "Mother Eagle and Father Eagle are coming back!"

One-Eye shimmied down the tree as fast as he could, with Eagle's Child clinging to his back, screeching protests. His friends helped knock the bird to the ground.

One hunter prepared an arrow to shoot at the approaching eagles. When they found their child, they would be fierce indeed.

"Forget about it!" One-Eye commanded. His face was bloody from the attack. "Something strange is happening." He dabbed at his good eye. "There's no luck for us here. This place has bad magic." He looked up at Aneze and blinked a few times.

"Let's get out of here."

So they left.

Aneze climbed out of the nest. She hid as best she could. She didn't want to draw Mother and Father Eagle's attention.

Down below, Eagle's Child was getting his first flying lesson. How else would he get back to the nest? His parents teased and taunted him with a fish—the meal they had brought home. He flapped and flapped. His parents kept the fish just out of reach. Poor Eagle's Child! What a long day he was having! Aneze knew what that was like.

She watched while he took his first short shaky flights—up to there—*oops*! That's the way. Now over to this branch—hang on now, take a break. Big leap up ahead, *flap, flap, flap*. That's it. Soon you'll be home and eating that fish.

Slowly, as Eagle's Child made his way up, Aneze climbed down. She kept clear of the family, but they were too busy to bother with her. She took it slowly. She was very wobbly, and it was a long way down. It had all happened so fast, going up. She took extra care not to slip. Under the tree she stretched out, flat on her back. Soon the shaking stopped. She felt better. She had escaped One-Eye again.

She closed her eyes. She wanted to talk with the old man. She really needed his advice.

"Do you think One-Eye will come back to get me?" she would ask him if he were here. But only the birds and the beetles were talking now. She sighed.

Then the answer came, except it was her own voice telling her, "You may cross paths again. But so far, you have beaten him every time."

Seal

ANEZE COULDN'T find them.

She would have to learn more about tracking. Were they looking for her? Maybe they thought she wanted to leave them. Maybe they thought she had gotten tired of being told what to do. Maybe they thought she had snuck off to be on her own again. Maybe they were happy she had left. She looked for the trapline. She looked for Aunt and Cub and the camp. She hadn't been watching when she followed Uncle and Ketch. She had just been following. She still had a lot to learn about being a hunter. They couldn't be far. Maybe they didn't want to be found.

She had to make camp by herself again. She ate fish from the lake. Aneze could handle herself alone. Maybe it was better this way. She didn't really fit in with people anyway. She was an orphan. She brought terrible luck. The hollow blew out like a fish bladder inside her. But she would get used to it. That night she made a fire and set up a lean-to as usual. She drank some hot water. The snow would be coming soon. Again. She shivered in her sealskin. Aunt had said she would help her sew a caribou suit. But she could do without it. She'd figure something out. Aneze drifted off to sleep.

She woke up suddenly. Snow had come. The forest was frozen. Ice covered each and every needle on the tree branches. They glittered. It was too bright. How could it be so bright? She hadn't slept that long, surely! She closed her eyes against the sharp shining needles. When she opened them again, the forest was gone.

She lay on ice with nothing beneath her sealskin. There was a hole beside her, into the water. She slipped into it. She slipped in because the water was her home. On the ice she flapped and flopped. But under water she was graceful and fast. She swam and swam without needing a breath. She swam toward one of her breathing holes. She made so many every winter. She poked her nose up into the hole and took a breath.

WHOOSH!

She was caught on a harpoon! It pricked her skin. She wriggled, but her wriggling just worked it deeper. She was pulled out of the water through her breathing hole. It was the old man! The old man was her hunter! She was so glad to see him again. She didn't even mind that he'd harpooned her.

"Oh, it's you," said the old man. He untied the harpoon line. "What a silly little seal you are." But he was gentle when he turned her over.

"You are not big enough for me to eat. Your skin is too thin and new for me to wear. Go back to your family, little one. Come and see me again when you are grown."

"But, Magician, my family is dead, remember?" Aneze-the-seal said.

The old man ignored her. He made cluck-cluck noises and tsk-tsk noises while he removed the harpoon from her chubby seal-body. He packed some ice into her wound.

"This water is good water. It's strong medicine," he said. "But you'll also need fire. Fire burns bad skin. Put the fire and some clean wood-ash in the wound. It will be all better."

Wood-ash? Why was he talking about wood-ash? There was no wood around here.

The old man pushed her back into the water. He looked all wavy and wobbly as she sank. She heard him call, "Go back to your family, Orphan Ahwak! Ai-ai, I didn't expect to see you so soon! Come back when you're grown, and we'll chat some more!"

But the old man didn't really fix her, because her seal-body wouldn't swim. She just dropped deeper, deeper and deeper into the water. It was getting dark down here. The blue of the surface was far away.

And then she was back in the forest. All the ice was gone. Lake water lapped against her fingertips. She had moved in the night. How far, she had no idea. She was very thirsty. She drank and drank until her belly was heavy.

"This water is good water," she said. The old man's voice came back to her. "It's strong medicine." Aneze emptied her water carrier and filled it with this new water.

Aneze

SHE COULD see the smoke through the trees. Could it be?

Since that peculiar dream, Aneze had been wandering around like a stunned blackfly. Then she had found one of Uncle's traps. Suddenly the wood looked familiar. She was able to walk to his next trap and the next. Now she remembered—she was almost at camp! Would they be happy to see her?

They weren't happy at all.

Aunt was sitting by the fire, her head sunk onto her arms. Aunt almost never sat and did nothing. Cub was trying to nuzzle his way under her tunic. He made a funny sound, "Mamamamam." He wanted to nurse, but Aunt ignored him. Uncle was stepping out of the tent. His face was gray. He looked old.

"What happened?" Aneze asked. "Where's Ketch?" Aunt and Uncle looked over to where she stood.

"Ahwak," Uncle said, "you came back." Aunt gazed at Aneze as if she didn't see anything. With one arm, she gathered Cub under her tunic. He stopped making his noise.

"Ketchwatin is sick," she said to the air around Aneze. "Lynx bit him." She turned back to stare at the ground again.

"Come here, come here." Uncle waved her over to the fire. "It's very bad. Spruce gum isn't working, and he can't drink any more tea. It's the fever from the bite. The wound has gone rotten." Uncle lowered his voice to a whisper. "He's leaving us. It won't be long now."

Leaving us! No!

Everything, it seemed to Aneze, everything was always changing—come and go, good-bye, hello. But not Ketch! Aneze couldn't bear that. Ketch mustn't change. He was solid, always the same. Everything turned out all right for him. He mustn't leave her.

"Can I see him?" She choked it out.

"You won't like it," Uncle warned.

That was fine. She already didn't like it.

She lifted the tent flap and ducked her head inside. *Pee-uu*! What was that stink? She coughed. Was that Ketch?

"Ketch-wa-tiiiiiin," she crooned, just to let him know that it was her, Aneze. She found a calfskin. She used her water carrier to soak it. She held it to her nose for a minute, until she got used to the air inside. She crouched down and crawled over to the hump in the sleeping furs. His breathing was shallow. It was too light and too fast. She pulled back the furs. He was on fire. This was not good! He was too old to get this hot. Only babies could stand it this hot. Ketch would melt.

"Here, Ketch, drink this. It's medicine water." Aneze tried to pour some into his mouth. "I know. I've used it myself. It's from a lake I was at. It's strong medicine." Ketch's eyelids twitched. Aneze placed the wet rag over his face. She pulled back the covers some more. There it was on his leg—the lynx bite. It had festered. Bad skin.

Uncle came into the tent. "We hunted Moose," he said from behind her. "Lynx must have been starving. He jumped—I don't know from where—he jumped onto Ketch's back. I whacked at him hard, but he took that chunk out first." Water dropped from Uncle's eyes. "Why couldn't Lynx have just waited a little while?"

He looked at Aneze. For a moment, she thought he really expected her to answer the question.

"We couldn't carry all that meat ourselves. There would have been plenty for everyone."

Aneze examined the bite. It was a bad wound. It oozed. She poured her water over it. "Uncle," she said, "maybe we should try to find that moss. You know, the moss that Cub had for his diapers? Maybe we could pack that in the bite. It might dry this up."

"I will look for some," Uncle said. "But the fever. It's the fever that's taking him fast."

"Let me try something," Aneze told him. "I have medicine. It's an idea. Maybe it will help. Please let me try."

Uncle squinted at Aneze. She tried to look wise and confident. Uncle shook his head.

"Do what you want, Ahwak girl. I know you care for him almost as much as I do." He turned to leave. "I'll get the moss."

Alone again with Ketch, Aneze tried to get him to drink. But she was just delaying the other thing. She didn't want to do the other thing. "Good water," the old man had said. "It's strong medicine. But what you need is fire. Fire burns bad skin." He had said that. She still didn't want to do it. "Put the fire and some clean wood-ash in the wound. It'll be all better."

She had to be brave. She poked her head out of the tent.

"Auntie, can you give me that stick there, from the fire? No, the long one with the coal on the end."

Aunt brought it over. Cub held on tightly to her skirts.

"Ahwak, what are you going to do? Your uncle says you are going to try some magic. What do you know about magic, Ahwak?" Aunt was scared of magic. But Aunt would do anything for Ketch. Her eyes opened so wide that she looked young, like a child. She looked like she wanted to believe, but all she could see was Orphan Ahwak.

"Auntie," Aneze said, "I know I'm just an orphan. And only a girl too. I know that." She took the burning stick from Aunt's hand.

"But…" Aneze sighed. She looked around for words that might help her aunt. "But maybe what Ketch needs right now…is an orphan girl…who knows a thing or two."

Aunt's face crumpled into a knot. Finally she nodded. And Aneze ducked back into the tent.

"Bye-bye, Ahwak!" She heard Cub's high voice calling from outside.

This is going to work, this is going to work just fine. It's going to be all right, Aneze told herself. She tried to tell this to Ketch too. She took the burning stick and made a small fire in the tent. Ketch didn't need any more heat right now, but he would soon if everything went well. She also needed the smoke—wood-smoke and plenty of ash.

Then she sang a little, just to let Ketch know that she was with him. That she was trying to help. Aneze was sure it would make a difference if he knew someone was on his side.

She had another look at the wound. It was on the fleshy part of his leg. That part was good. She was sure she shouldn't burn his bone. That couldn't be right. She poured medicine water all around the area. She let it dry in the smoky air.

She sang some more, to let Ketch know that she didn't want to hurt him. But they had to chase away the sickness together. She sang to ask him to be brave and strong. She sang for herself too. Then she carefully selected the first stick, the one that started the fire. Its end glowed hot. Little sparks wiggled across black ash. She sat across Ketch's leg to hold it down. She sang one last verse.

Fish lakes of fish—stay near
Hunt woods with beasts—stay near
Wear the clothes your mother mends
Catch the spear your father sends
Sing again with your best friend
Stay, Ketchwatin—stay here

Aneze drove the fire stick into Ketch's wound. The hump in the furs lurched and moaned. She held on to him and kept her mind clear. She must get every part of the bite or all his pain would be wasted. The burnt stick crumbled as she turned and twisted it all around the bite. Sweat poured into her eyes. It was so hard to see in here. Was that Ketch who was shaking so hard? Was it her?

There! Done.

Ai, it's all done. Aneze threw the stick away. Horrible stick! It skittered to the tent wall. She scrambled to get another clean calfskin and soaked it with the medicine water. She packed this into the wound. Then she sat down by his head.

"Now," she ordered, "you come back." She jammed the water carrier between his teeth. "You don't leave, and I won't leave either. Neither of us leaves, all right?"

And this time Ketchwatin drank. He drank the medicine water.

Yes, good, he agrees, Aneze thought. He agrees not to leave.

After a while, Ketch stopped burning. In fact he felt cold and clammy. Aneze stirred up the fire and heaped the furs on him. She left the water carrier by the bed in case he got thirsty. She would go back to the lake for more medicine water. He would be weak for a while.

"Soon you'll need soup," Aneze said. "You need to warm up again." She got up. She had a cramp.

She must have been sitting for a long time. She crawled
out of the tent.

They were all waiting outside: Aunt, Uncle, Cub.
Aneze felt very tired, but she gave them all a big smile.
The fever had run away, scared by the hotter fire.
Ketch was going to be all right.

"Papa got diaper-moss for you, Ahwak," Cub said.
Aunt and Uncle said nothing. But their faces shone on
her like the sun.

Aunt reached out and held Aneze very tight. Just
like she was Cub's size and not a great big girl.

"Ahwak, you did it? You did it! Ketch is really
going to be all right!" Aneze let herself be hugged, even
though she felt shy. Aunt was so happy Ketch was going
to stay. They were all so happy because of something
Aneze did. She felt a little bit proud.

THE FIRE WAS heating up the stones, and Aunt was
plucking a grouse for the pot. Ketch sat near the fire. Its
warmth kept the wind out of his bones. Ketch could walk
again, but he still had to be careful. Cub was playing with
Ketch's slingshot, trying to hit a tree with his stone.

"There it goes, you got it—ooohhh, almost!" Ketch
cried. "That tree is too skinny. Try another." He winked
at Aneze.

Aneze placed a marten skin to dry by the fire—not too close though, or the skin would be hard and useless.

Aunt stopped her work to watch Ketch. She gazed at him with soft eyes and a half smile on her face. Aunt did that often, ever since Ketch had grown strong enough to leave the tent. "Ketchwatin, don't let Cub tire you out," she said.

Uncle stood by, sniffing the air. "Next light it will be time to go."

It was time to travel to the barren ground. It was time to meet Caribou.

Aneze didn't know what to think. She was returning to the barren ground! It was sad to remember the last time she had been there, when the old man had left her. It was even worse to think of the time before, when he had first found her under the snow.

But now she was traveling with others; she wasn't alone anymore. And they would meet more people along the way. Then there would be news and games and feasts—everything was going to be just like it had always been! She thought back to the last time she traveled to the barren ground with Mother, Father and Brother.

No, that wasn't right. Everything was going to be different. Even Aneze was different. It could never be like it had been before.

"I'll just walk out to a few traps before we go."
Uncle shouldered his bow.

"Wait!" Aunt cried. She brushed feathers off her
tunic and rushed into the tent. She came back out
holding Aneze's bow and hunting knife.

"Maybe Ahwak would like to join you," she
suggested.

How astonishing! Aunt didn't like Aneze to go
hunting.

But Aunt was looking down on Aneze with soft
eyes. A little smile was on her face. Aunt was being
kind! Aneze felt her own eyes smart. She looked around,
not sure what to do. Uncle gave her a nod.

"Why not?" he said. "Ahwak is a good hunting
partner, and I could use the help."

Aneze blinked hard as she scrambled up. She didn't
want to start crying—what a silly thing to do! She took
her hunting gear from Aunt with her head bowed.
But when she looked up, she tried a trembling smile
for everyone—for Aunt, Uncle, Cub and Ketch.

"My name," she told them all, "is Aneze."

AUTHOR'S NOTE

TO IMAGINE a character like Orphan Ahwak, I needed first to do some reading. I started reading biographies about extraordinary Inuit women such as Ada Blackjack and Anauta. I also read histories of the Arctic, of exploration and of the early fur trade as it reached Manitoba and Saskatchewan. As I discovered my lead character and her unique adventure, the story took me into other reading: books on animals, plants, geography, archaeology, anthropology. My notes show one checklist after another, scribbled down as I wrote the story. The lists were full of questions such as: Would Mother keep her children if forced to marry Watonbee? Were kayaks likely made from driftwood *and* bone? How are beaver dams constructed? All were questions to be answered online or at the library, if possible.

I decided that Orphan Ahwak, or more correctly Aneze, came from a people who traveled the northern edges of the boreal forest of what is now known as western Canada. I imagined that Aneze's people, based on my reading on the Dene and the Chippewa, had not yet encountered European traders. I imagined the people to the south, based on my reading on the Woodland Cree, had also not yet begun significant trading, as evidenced by Aneze's "enemies'" lack of firearms.

Especially helpful was the Dene elders' project *They Will Have Our Words,* edited by Lynda Holland and Mary Ann Kkailther. A great source of historical color and inspiration was explorer Samuel Hearne's journal entries (as selected by Farley Mowat in *Coppermine Journey,* and appearing in Ken McGoogan's *Ancient Mariner*). In 1770, Dene leader Matonabbee led Samuel Hearne on more than 3,500 miles of hard overland travel to find the Northwest Passage.

The old man's culture is based mostly on my reading of Asen Balikci's book *The Netsilik Eskimo.* The Netsilingmiut inhabit the region around Boothia Peninsula and King William Island, Nunavut.

However, I did take liberties with the historical record. The old man's kayak-roll technique is taken from the Greenlander kayak roll. Similar kayak rolls are practiced in Alaska. There is no record of such in-kayak rolls being performed along the Canadian Arctic coast. But it could be presumed that the technique migrated from West to East, along with early Inuit peoples. And even if kayak rolling was no longer practiced among the old man's people, I decided that a hunter as wise and cultivated as the old man would surely be aware of it (through his travels, or his dreams perhaps). I imagined he would teach it to his sons, and to Aneze, as an intelligent (and enjoyable) safety precaution.

Any nomadic group that was familiar with the Barren Grounds (of what is now Nunavut and the Northwest Territories) would have likely had encounters with Inuit people. But these Inuit would have been inland tundra dwellers, not coastal people like the old man. For the sake of the story, Aneze had to experience an entirely different world, where little would seem ordinary or recognizable. To do this, I transported her what would be a superhuman distance in record time. Whether she covered this distance herself, whether the old man happened to be traveling far from his territory, or whether he learned of her and went to collect her by magic, I leave for you to decide. Myself, I'd say the magic theory is the most plausible.

When necessary, I referred to individual animals as "he." I did this for clarity only, since Aneze was a "she." If only our English language had a personal pronoun that didn't refer to gender, but also had a personal ring to it. Aneze would never consider calling an animal "it."

Obviously *Orphan Ahwak* is written from imagination, not experience. People, wildlife and landscapes have been dreamed up and then made as true as possible through research at the McGill University libraries, Concordia libraries and the Bibliotheque Nationale. At times I had to synthesize what I thought to be a plausible scenario, based on a variety of sources. And since the book is set three hundred-odd years ago, it was not always possible to find definitive answers. Also, because I was trying to engage today's readers, there were moments when I consciously colored my portrait of Aneze and her story with a contemporary slant. (As opposed to all the unconscious times I've no doubt done it.) Aneze's treatment of Ketch's wound is one example; when she refers to her heart as the seat of her feelings is another.

Having said all that, I sincerely hope I've written no egregious errors into the book. No reader deserves to be yanked harshly out of the world of a story just because the author allowed her ignorance to show.

My hope was to write a gripping story about a courageous young spirit in an astoundingly challenging environment—a spirit who is much like other young spirits I'm lucky to know, even if their challenging environments are very different today. If reading *Orphan Ahwak* is even half as enjoyable as writing it was, then its work is done.

Thanks for reading.
Raquel Rivera

RAQUEL RIVERA is an artist and writer who has written three children's books. She has lived in Barcelona, Singapore and Kuala Lumpur, but now makes her home in Montreal, Quebec, with her husband and two children.